William T. Meloy

Wanderings in Europe

William T. Meloy

Wanderings in Europe

ISBN/EAN: 9783337194147

Printed in Europe, USA, Canada, Australia, Japan

Cover: Foto ©Andreas Hilbeck / pixelio.de

More available books at **www.hansebooks.com**

CONTENTS.

vho did not want to be taken across the waters, to go
)n shore. The plank was pulled out; the officers, in
)right attire, were in their places, and the steamer
)egan to move out from the pier. Then we lost sight
)f individual forms, but over the crowd there
eemed to be a myriad of white doves brooding low.
:t was our friends waving their handkerchiefs.
These signals were exchanged even when we were so
ar out that it was impossible to determine who it was
hat lingered there with the eye strained to get the
ast glimpse of the outgoing ship.

For the first time I fully realized that I was going
broad, and that the waters of the Atlantic must be
:rossed and recrossed before I could see the loved
)nes of home and church. Those who have often had
his experience lose the exquisite pain that stimulates
he action of the heart, and gives a sort of ecstasy to
he parting hour. It is a loss. The boy loses much
vhen he speaks so often that he is no longer embar-
·assed as he makes his address. He may feel more of
:omfort, when the embarrassment and excitement are
;one, but his audience may feel far less of interest.
'How did you feel when you left the shore ?" " How
lid you feel when you lost sight of land ?" One can not
vell answer. Ask the preacher how he felt when he
lelivered his first sermon. Ask the physician how he
'elt when he saw his first patient. Ask the lawyer

how he felt when he first said in court, "May the Court please and Gentlemen of the jury." Ask your brother-in-law how he felt when at the twilight he told your sister his story of love, and solicited her hand. Of course they can not tell. There are some things to be enjoyed but once. You may have the same happenings again, but the same enjoyment—never. A speech, or visit, or proposal that does not have a little of the first emotion in it, will be dull and spiceless.

But the care of seeing that my trunk is in "34," and the worry of adjusting myself to live in a six-by-five room with a physician, whose down-town offices occupy more space than would be given to a hundred people on shipboard, bade all sentimental reflections "down," and unlike "Banquo's" ghost, they downed. You make up your mind to compel your body to be comfortable in discomfort. You imagine that the little shelf on which you are to sleep, will be a real luxury, since you are to be "rocked in the cradle of the deep." It is but little longer, and no wider, than the shelf on your dining-room sideboard; but here you are to spend more than seven nights, without enough air to last a deep-breathing mortal for two hours, and even that supply liable to be cut off if it becomes necessary to close the ports.

Outward bound, we quickly pass Bartholdi's costly statue of "Liberty Enlightening the World," pass the island where our ragged Ohio regiments landed in war time, when we were called from the front to suppress disloyalty in New York City, pass the old fort where political prisoners were held—out—out until the land is seen no more.

"Why did you not stand by me and see the pilot leave the vessel? You have lost your last chance of getting back to Chicago! It is too late now to repent. You must go with me!" The voice was that of my companion, Dr. Charles Gilbert Davis, of Chicago. He is the first person to whom I will introduce you, and that you may know how highly favored I was in having his company, his portrait has been secured for this book. The fact is, he was taking me with him, and he little imagined what a charge he had to keep, until it was too late for him to repent.

We are in a new world. It is to be our home for eight days. We can hear nothing more from the continents of earth than we can from the planet Mars. We are really nearer Mars, for we can see it every night. In the new condition of things, we begin to look about to see what sort of beings inhabit this new world. Who are to be our neighbors? A dozen of them are from Chicago. We were too busy to know much about each other there, but here we have ample time to talk about our business and family descent, always leaving out the grand-uncles who came to

America to escape the halter. We had often seen some of these neighbors. We had hurried past them on the streets of the city with a " good morning," or a grunt, just as we had much or little time for civilities. Here is a learned Judge, who, although on the shady side of sixty, has taken to himself a charming widow of twelve years standing. To see them wrapped up in their blankets, with their steamer chairs close together, one would think they were lovers of sixteen. Near them is a millionaire with his family. He is a great-hearted fellow who despises formality, and delights in horrifying English gentlemen by telling them that he is a " baker." Wherever he went he did not hesitate to tell the people of the superiority of America over any country in Europe. Through Mrs. F——, who is a lady of wonderful refinement, I was introduced to the entire party, and we soon learned more of each other than we would have done had we lived as neighbors for a century in Chicago.

There is but little going on to talk about for the first few days on the ocean, so we drift into personal history with an occasional divergence into the regions of philosophy, or poetry, or theology, or politics. But as we get acquainted with our new surroundings, we take up the old land themes. Our food and servants, and our neighbor's dress, and other people's business in general, occupy our leisure hours. Some people settle down and try to read, but interruptions are so frequent that I have noticed a passenger with the same page of the book open day after day, only when a page back of the one usually opened, had been referred to, so as to get the connection. The little ocean community numbered, all told, six hundred and twenty-two, but from some of these we were as rigidly separated by the rules of the vessel as men are divided by caste in China. They were second-cabin passengers.

At eleven o'clock the first day out, seats at table were assigned us. My lot fell next to a Roman Catholic priest. He was fat and jolly; freely offered absolution to everybody for everything they said or did. He was well fed, and if liquor would have made him so, might have been well drunk. Beer and wine, with an occasional stronger cup, freshened up his spirits and gave vigor to his conversation. Four meals and two or three extra luncheons were served every day. Many people ate as though they had never had a good square meal in all their lives before. Then they struggled up on deck, and, wrapped up like mummies in their steamer chairs, folded their arms and waited till, under the mysterious operations of nature, the luxuries of the table were transformed into blood. Others paced the deck from one end to the other, as though bent on some great enterprise.

Among these, a young Englishman walked bareheaded and resolute. A gentleman who had at one time some presidential aspirations, could be seen at almost any hour from daylight until ten o'clock at night, hurrying along the deck, yet making as little progress in getting anywhere as he did in getting to the White House. A young officer of the English army also was a distinguished deck-walker, and for some reason always kept the legs of his trousers rolled up, as one would do if walking through the mud. But possibly the meager wages that England pays her soldiers required that he should only wear out one part of his clothes at a time. Yet on a quiet voyage

> To-day is so like yesterday
> We take the lying sister for the same.

One morning I was rewarded for early-rising by the sight of two whales, which came near the vessel and revealed their true nature—as some men do—by spouting freely. The doctor said that they were only porpoises, but fortunately other early-risers were with me to testify. Is it not strange that to a man who has not risen early enough to see it, a whale is only a porpoise? I am not inclined to moralize overmuch, but on land I have heard many people talk the same way about other things. The fox said, "sour grapes." A man says, "only a porpoise!"

After this, the inhabitants of our floating island began to be interested in the lower orders of creation. The fact that whales had been seen was telegraphed over the community, and all began looking for whales. We saw much that otherwise we would never have seen. An occasional dolphin delighted us with his graceful swimming. Porpoises by the hundred plunged along the sides of the vessel, like men in a circus tumbling for our amusement. The nautilus, best of sailors, set himself to float in our direction, and though occasionally turned over by the rude waves, soon righted himself and went on his course, drifting, like many on life's great ocean, not knowing whither. "Whither!" I wonder if Professor Briggs noticed one of these before adopting his loose theology and writing his book. But, like the nautilus, the professor has probably discovered that even successful "drifting" requires some skill. As we stood by the prow of the vessel, the flying-fish rose in considerable numbers. My impression, from looking at the dried specimen, was that he only jumped. But he does much more. He darts from the waves like an arrow flying from the bow, rises a few feet above the water, and vigorously flapping his silvery wings, takes his flight away from real or imagined danger. When he feels himself safe, or when he is wearied by being too long out of his element, he buries himself like a flash of light in the sea again. He remains out of the water probably half a minute, and flies at his best about six hundred feet. These fish are preyed on by dolphins, sharks, and gulls. Their lives are in constant peril. David's figure of the partridge on the mountains might have been as striking if he had used the flying-fish of the ocean, but people would not have been so well acquainted with it.

The little petrel came to visit us in mid-ocean. Many surmisings were expressed as to how the birds rested at night, where they hatched their young, and on what they fed. The children have called them " Mother Carey's chickens." The name is a diminutive of Peter, and the light skimming motion of the birds over the water was supposed to represent Peter's walking on the waves. The name was illy chosen, for Peter never had faith enough to be at home on the waves as these birds are, and the rougher the waters the more at home the birds seem to be. They hatch their brood on the rocks, and when they are old enough take the whole family to sea. When they want to sleep, they simply tuck their heads under their wings and lie down on the waves, without any care where they may be when morning comes. They are ocean tramps, waiting at the back door of the ship to get what the household does not want, and then moving on, are as much at home one place as another. The sailors dread their appearance, believing that their coming always presages a storm. Their lives are stormy, but they seem to live with much of inward peace.

One day I was standing alone at the prow of the ship, looking for flying-fish, or whatever might show itself in the waters, when a hand was laid on my shoulder. I turned and saw a gentleman of some sixty summers, who immediately extended his hand saying, "I want to know you."

"That is the privilege of all good-looking men and women who have the good taste to desire it," I replied.

His home is in Lynchburg, Virginia. We soon found out that we had fought against each other in the War of the Rebellion. He was with the South in the conflict, and I with the North. We also discovered that we had been on opposing sides in several battles. Here was a new theme for conversation, and we entered on it. In a short time I discovered what a noble nature had opposed me. He presented me to his wife, and I wondered if she would be as cordial as her husband had been. I determined to spring the mine at once and test her graces.

"Madam, are you not glad that when I shot at your husband in the Valley of Virginia, I was so poor a marksman? You might have been a widow— at least for a few years."

She did not sneer; she seemed not even to regard my attempt at wit, but answered, "Truly I am sir, and you will permit me to say that I thank God he was equally unskillful when he returned the shot." My new-made friend is a tobacco merchant, and proposed to ship me enough to last me for years. But I do not use tobacco, so I gave him my father's address and he agreed to make the offering to him. My father is not a preacher, and the vote of the church was in favor of large liberty in behalf of the eldership. But the old strife is forgotten and the old bitterness has died out of such noble natures as those of Major and Mrs. Winfree.

But while I conversed with my friends, the doctor came up and positively affirmed that he had seen two whales on the opposite side of the ship.

"Only porpoises, my son," I replied. His boomerang came home to him sooner than he anticipated. But he had witnesses, and the only thing left for me was to say that they could not have been so large as mine were. Why is it that on the sea, as well as on the land, we are so careful to make others feel comfortable and contented? Is it because we are so easily satisfied with what we have, and minify our neighbor's good in order to keep up an exact equality, or possibly gain a little superiority? True, neither of us owned the whales we had seen, but we had seen them and that

2

gave us a sort of propriety in them. They were ours just as much, and more, than the possessions of earth are which we may have a title to, but which we have never seen and which we can never enjoy.

As if to relieve the monotony, an occasional sail was seen, and at long intervals a steamer came in sight. One of the latter signaled us that she had seen icebergs. An iceberg is an interesting thing to read about. It brings with it a sort of chilly atmosphere that does not give promise of a pleasant meeting. We had only received this intelligence a few hours when we had our first experience of a fog. It was so dense that we could see but a few yards across the waters. Watchers were promptly on the lookout. The hoarse-throated horn sounded its warnings every two minutes, yet with the noise of the machinery and the waves, it was doubted whether the horn could be heard very much farther than we could see. Disagreeable as the sound of the fog-horn was, in itself, it was sweet as the voice of soft recorders to us, for it meant safety from collision with other vessels. But if an iceberg were encountered, there could be no protection. Our fog-horn would not warn it off. There is nothing at sea that is more dreaded than a fog. There may be no real danger, but there can be no assurance of safety. Let us have a dead calm, a stiff breeze, a violent storm, anything rather than a fog. We dread icebergs.

They are cold and uninviting. Some people are like icebergs. You do not want to be near them. You do not want them to be near you. After awhile they may drift into the warm gulf stream of love and be subdued; but until that time comes, you need not cultivate their presence. And especially do we avoid them in a fog, when the way is uncertain.

The horn sounds less frequently. Are the watchers growing careless? Not at all. The clouds are lifting and the sunlight is seen on the sea. It has grown quite clear, and you can see an object ten miles distant. The fog-horn has ceased to blow. Its noise would be very offensive now that there is no danger. The note of warning, in time of peril, is to be desired, but some people are never so happy as when sounding the fog-horn under a clear sky, and over a calm sea. They attribute their morbidness to their faithfulness.

CHAPTER II.

THE sight of land caused considerable excitement in our little community, and the decks were soon crowded. We had seen land all our lives, until within the last few days, but passengers looked out at it with as much eagerness as though they had never seen it before. The rocky sentinels that guard the southern coast of Ireland were hailed in the distance, and I confess to have shared in the general sentiment, and silently thanked God that He had made the dry land as well as the wide and deep sea. We lost all interest in the monsters of the deep and feasted our hungry eyes on the evergreen hills of old Ireland. Field-glasses were in demand, and light-houses were as carefully inspected as though we had never seen a lantern in all our life-time.

"Home Rule" was the subject of earnest conversation. We were to be in Europe for two months, and we must begin to take an interest in European politics. The Irish priest came on deck and grew jubilant as he looked on his native land again, and

(20)

talked with enthusiasm of the beauties of Tipperary. Within a half mile of us lay the wreck of the *City of Chicago.* The upper deck and rigging were above water. This unfortunate vessel, in the midst of a dense fog, had run directly against a rocky bank more than one hundred feet high. She had gotten out of her course, and while the watch were looking toward the left side for the light-house, she had veered so far to the left that the light-house was in advance and to the right. The ship was therefore steered directly against the cliff. Providentially, it was ordered that no rock was encountered until within a ship length of the cliff, and then she ran on a narrow shelving rock that held her from sinking. Had the vessel gone thirty feet either to the right or left, she must have gone down, and the loss of life would have been frightful. As it was, passengers and crew were saved, although the former lost most of their baggage. Forty thousand bushels of wheat were in her hold. The life-boats were manned, and most of the ladies got in them to be drifted about in the darkness for several hours. Others, however, escaped up the cliff by means of rope ladders. To them the darkness was an aid, for they could not see their peril, and made the ascent with comparative ease. Many of the ladies exhibited true American grit, and did not show the least nervousness as they left the boat for their gloomy ride.

I met a party of six under the care of Miss Halsted, of Yonkers, New York, who showed the spirit of courage in the midst of difficulties. One young lady of the party is a fine violinist and refused to part with her violin at the demand of a sailor. She simply clutched it under her arm, saying, "It does not weigh anything and I will keep it with me." After four hours, the party were landed at the foot of a high hill, up which they climbed on their hands and knees, the bright young violinist still clinging to her precious fiddle. After walking two miles to a little village, they were somewhat refreshed, but presented a very undignified appearance with torn and muddy dresses, water-soaked shoes, disheveled hair, and hands and faces that told how earnestly they had climbed. Bangs were at a discount, ruffles were rags, soap and water were luxuries. The party took the first train to Belfast, where they secured "hand-me-down" dresses, hastily trimmed other hats, and were off on their tour of the continent with as much zeal as though nothing unusual had happened them.

At Queenstown many of our passengers left us, being taken off by a small tender that came alongside and received passengers and their luggage without stopping our ship. Our little community was being broken up. We parted from some of them with regret, with uttered prayers, and the warm pressure of honest hands. Then the ropes were unfastened, and the little boat and great steamer drifted apart, attended by the usual waving of hats and handkerchiefs.

The decks were thinned. We missed our friends, and the rest of the voyage was simply a looking for the end. How much like life it is! The world is never quite the same to us when our dear ones have left us; the skies never seem so bright, flowers have lost something of their perfume, and music does not cheer our hearts as of old. All may be as bright and sweet, but somehow we lose the capacity for enjoyment, and think more of the end. We learned that a fearful storm had prevailed on this part of the sea the day before; while with us, a few hundred miles west, all was placid and calm. The truth of the report was soon confirmed, for we passed by a splendid vessel that had been driven on the rocks, and was even now being broken to pieces by the waves. Three brave fellows lost their lives in attempting to take off the crew. The path of safety was very narrow, but the vessel that had outridden many a storm could not be controlled, and was driven on the rocks. We can never argue that because dangers have been avoided we will surely come off safely from the next ones that threaten us.

It was noon when we arrived at Liverpool, and in the confusion of disembarking and looking after our

trunks (you must call them "boxes"), formal "good-
byes" were not generally spoken. The custom-house
officers seemed careful in proportion to the unwilling-
ness of the passenger to have his boxes examined. A
minister had to pay a fine for carrying too many
cigars for a preacher to smoke. With all her talk of
free trade, England does not admit American tobacco
without a heavy duty.

Our little family was now entirely broken up,
and by ones and twos spread over the land, going,
like the children of Noah, wherever their inclination
prompted, to meet occasionally, as we journeyed,
and pass a hurried word or two in regard to the
voyage over and the time of return. We spent but
little time in Liverpool. Everything appeared to
be solid and permanent. The docks of the city are the
wonder of the world. They cover a space of four
hundred acres of water along the Mersey. A hasty
glance at these, or a small part of them, and we are
on the way to the "booking" office.

For the first time we find use for the old table of
our childhood—£, s., d. It is exceedingly awkward,
and my examination of the accuracy of the change
given me must have been amusing or annoying to the
agent. It is difficult to tell whether some Englishmen
are amused or annoyed at you, for in both cases they
are as sober and solemn as the grave. We have a

double process to go through. We calculate the amount in pounds, shillings, and pence, and see that our change is correct, and then, to satisfy ourselves as to the cost of what we have purchased, have to reduce it all back again to dollars and cents. It is like studying our arithmetic over again. But I had resolved to do all in a thorough manner. Accordingly, I at once began to say "ha'penny" and "tuppence," and "tuppence ha'penny," as glibly as though I had been brought up in an English candy store.

The first annoyance was to get our boxes "booked." I asked for a check, and the agent, after exacting "tuppence" for it, gave me a little scrap of paper, the stub of which had been pasted on the box.

"Is it necessary for me to see that my box is put in the car?"

"Naw."

"Will it be necessary for me to look after it by the way?"

"Naw!"

"Will I find it at the station at Stratford on the arrival of the train?"

"Certainly. Have you never been away from home before?"

That rebuke quieted me, and we hurried to the cars. If quick-witted men had been put to work to invent the worst possible system of railroading—a system that would insure the least accommodation to the traveler and the greatest possible discomfort and insecurity, and at the same time the most expensive arrangement for the company—they could not have hit on a happier invention than an English railway. The cars themselves are ridiculously small, and are divided up into little compartments that will hold ten persons. You are locked in, without water, or any possibility of getting out, until the next stop is made, and the guard comes and unlocks the door. You may happen to be closeted with a maniac or robber, but you must stay in the company that has been selected for you. When night comes, a man walks along the top of the car and drops down a dim old lamp through an opening in the roof, near which it hangs, shedding on the top of your head its sickly light.

Tickets are examined before you are put in the compartment, or shortly afterward, and are not generally taken up until you arrive at your destination, and then the door is opened and the conductor takes them from you. On several occasions the train was stopped a mile or two out in the country, for the sole purpose of allowing the conductor to collect the tickets. Imagine such a thing in America! When we arrived at Stratford, our boxes were not there. I took occasion

to tell the station agent what I thought of English
railroads. He was polite and listened attentively
while I told him of the assurances of the Liverpool
agent. He apologized as well as he could and at once
telegraphed along the line to find the boxes. His
search was successful and the next train brought them
to us. But in many cases you can not even book the
boxes in this way. The road assumes no responsi-
bility. A little tab is pasted on the trunk, and it is
well for you to see that it is put on the cars, and you
must be on hands to claim it when the train stops.
But sometimes, in a long train where cars have been
switched about, you can not tell where the box may be,
and you have the delight of crowding along from one
end of the platform to the other, looking at the luggage of five hundred passengers before you can pick
out your own. There is no bell-rope attached to the
cars for the conductor's use. He carries a little whistle
about his neck, and with this signals the engineer
when to move his train. We took frequent occasion
to ridicule these things, and wondered why the East
stupidly refused to learn from the West. A look of
incredulity was apparent when we spoke of our sleeping, drawing-room, dining, and parlor cars, with a
stenographer and type-writer and waiting-maid, and
barber shop and bath-room attachment.

But there are some things we might learn from the East, and which we should learn. Human life is more sacred than it is with us. People are not allowed to walk across or along the tracks of the railway. At every station there is a way either above or beneath the tracks, by which to get from one side of the road to the other, and as a result of this, it seldom happens that anyone loses his life by being run down by an engine.

The railway companies vie with each other in keeping the property that belongs to them in good order. The grass along the sides of the track is neatly cut, and at every station you will see, in summer time, flower beds in perfect order. Vines, well trained, are creeping about the doorways. Great roses, of varied color and sweet perfume, give an idea of Paradise itself.

England is a beautiful country. Its farms are like gardens and lawns. Everything about its rural life gives the impression of carefulness and industry. It has a finished look that is in marked contrast with the great half-cultivated grain fields of the West. Its home life, if we may judge from external surroundings, is peculiarly happy. There is no rush at table, such as we are accustomed to in America. The Englishman takes plenty of time to eat and sleep and extend good fellowship to his neighbor. As I looked at stately dwellings and lowly cottages, the words of Mrs. Hemans were recalled.

The free, fair homes of England !
Long, long, in hut and hall,
May hearts of native proof be reared
To guard each hallowed wall !
And green forever be the groves,
And bright the flowery sod,
Where first the child's glad spirit loves
Its country and its God ! "

CHAPTER III.

IT was evening time when we reached Stratford-on-Avon, the birthplace of Shakespeare, the immortal. A quaint old town it truly is, but its streets are well paved and scrupulously clean. The citizens have a sort of self-respect and local pride born of veneration for the great poet. We lodged at the Shakespeare house, an old inn with seven gables. Part of the old tavern which William visited too often, remains intact. The proprietress of this hotel is shrewd enough to make everything about it savor of Shakespeare. Every room is named after one of the characters prominent in his plays. "Take this gentleman up to 'King Lear's' room" said the clerk. "Take that gentleman to 'Timon of Athens'' room." On the door was the name of the character. I sat down, drew a long breath, and thought of the wreck that Ignatius Donnelly was trying to make. We visited the house where William was born, and examined the butcher shop, where, for a time, he helped his father. His dramatic talents must have been developed very early in life, and under peculiarly trying conditions. It is recorded of him that even in killing a calf he was tragical, and attended the blood-letting with a speech. We also visited his grave in the church at Stratford, and read the inscription on the slab, which has so often been quoted :

Good friend, for Jesus's sake forbear
To dig the dust inclosed here.
Blest be the man that spares these stones,
And curst be he that moves my bones.

Leaving the old church, I came out into the grounds, where there is a fine bronze statue erected to his memory. On the sides of the pedestal there are several extracts from his writings. The reading of these excited in my mind a desire to repeat parts of his plays, with which I used, in younger days, to be famil-iar. I mounted a corner of the base stone and began. The doctor looked at me as though he were either dis-gusted with my display of myself or envious of my tragic skill. I could not determine which. The workmen noticed me and came near. The keepers, loafers, and sight-seers gathered about me. I had an audience and became still more tragic. The doctor looked worried by the attention I was attract-ing. He had a reputation to keep up at home if I had not. "What will the fellow do next, I wonder?"

he muttered, and motioned for me to come away. But my audience was increasing in size and the interest was growing. I repeated the words of Prince Henry over the slain body of Percy, "Ill-weaved ambition, how much art thou shrunk, etc." The doctor's mortification was growing in exact proportion to the interest I was exciting. Then a happy thought struck him. If I had humiliated him and sinned against his dignity, he would have revenge. He joined the group of listeners. I had captured him, too! But he gently tapped his head with his hand, and getting the eyes of my audience, looked sideways at me, and tapped his head again, saying, "You need not be alarmed at him. He is generally harmless. I am traveling with him and thought he was cured of these spells, but this morning he got away from the hotel, and I find him here. You can quietly listen to him until he wears himself out. Do not make any demonstration and he will be easily controlled. I will get him to the hotel again." I did not know just what the doctor was saying, but somehow my audience lost interest. The magnetic chain of sympathy between us was broken. I quit speaking, and then my friend came forward, and without a word, took my arm and led me away. I noticed that my former audience opened the way for us, and made no demonstration whatever. We walked away as quietly as though we were being taken to our own funerals. When we got out of sight and hearing, he confessed all except his mortification at the free exhibition I had been giving.

We have found out that the people here seldom laugh. They do not understand jokes, and so we have arranged that we will laugh at each other's witticisms, though we may have heard them repeated a dozen times before.

We were next driven to Anne Hathaway's cottage. In Shakespeare's house we saw the very niche in the chimney where William used to sit and dry his feet after his excursions into the premises of Sir Thomas Lucey. I have the pleasure of giving the reader a good picture of the Hathaway cottage, with its thatched roof. In it is the old red bench where he and Anne sat together and whispered words of love. The bench bears the marks of William's penknife, and it is probable that, during moments of embarrassment, he chipped the bench on which they sat, without any consciousness of the indelicacy of his conduct. But as Anne was twenty-six years old, she could easily forgive the rudeness of a lover of eighteen. I sat down on the old bench and tried to imagine the style of William's courtship, but the room was full of visitors, and the imagination was no wilder than on ordinary occasions.

3

The cottage was in the possession of an old lady, the only living descendant of the Hathaways, who spoke of her honored kindred with great reverence. We dropped a shilling into her hand. Somehow people in England always keep the palms of their hands up when they meet you. But she generously plucked a few pansies and gave them to us, reminding us that they grew in the yard at the Hathaway cottage.

Some Chicagoans came here early in the year 1892, and, whether in fun or earnest, I know not, proposed to buy the cottage to take to Chicago. The corporation of Stratford became alarmed. They at once purchased the old building, paying for it three thousand pounds. The old place was not worth five dollars, and it could not possibly have been removed to America. The thatched roof would have been pulverized before getting it to Liverpool. But the proposal brought a neat little fortune to the old lady, and she can live the rest of her days in comfort. The corporation have, since our visit, taken possession of the place, and will get their sweet revenge by charging everyone a sixpence that cares to see the old bench and bedstead. I laughingly told some of the authorities that it would not have been possible to take the cottage so far in its dilapidated condition, but they replied that Chicago wanted the earth and everything on it and under it, and that they were

ANNE HATHAWAY'S COTTAGE.

determined they would have to get it all before they could take away the cottage.

I left Stratford regretfully. The authorship of Shakespeare's plays is a matter of dispute. It would be esteemed a blasphemy to utter a doubt here where he lived. But someone did write a book with wonderful skill. It reveals an intimate knowledge of the higher revelation in which the workings of the human heart are explained. It is a book that both ennobles and debases. It went on its mission and still lives. It will be handed down through the centuries, and by coming ages regarded as it is to-day, the most wonderful production of the human brain, undirected by the inbreathings of the Spirit of God.

It is but a short ride from Stratford to Warwick. Here we were to see the first substantial castle, though I had been building castles all my life. Those who built these great castles of stone were more foolish, for they cost much more labor than the sort we build with so much enthusiasm in our youth. The feudal lord must have both his substance and his subjects protected. He must have a fort to which he could resort, and where, even after defeat, he could bid defiance to his victorious enemies. Those who have fallen heir to these castles and the estates connected therewith, have in some instances improved and beautified them, but in others they have been unable to keep them in repair, and they have fallen into ruins. Warwick Castle has been so well preserved that no one should miss a visit to it when in England. Look at the frowning walls and towers before you enter. Look at the outside before you have seen the inside, and then take another look at the walls after you have been within them. Let us enter. The door that now swings in the arched way was not originally there. Look up at the stone archway and you will see the teeth or pointed spears of the grim old portcullis that tell of disappointed enemies and a garrison, safe, because the portcullis was dropped a moment before they reached the walls. Many acres are inclosed, and here and there in the walls the towers rise where the defenders of the castle assembled, and through long narrow openings shot their arrows and hurled darts at their enraged enemies. Within these towers, some of which are one hundred and forty feet in height, are narrow stone stairways, the steps of which have been worn by the feet of the old warriors and the new visitors.

In these towers, too, are guard-rooms, where the watchers and fighters could retire, and where many a wounded man has received what care the skill of the time could bestow. Beneath these towers, or in deep vaults, are the dungeons where unfortunate prisoners were left to live or die, the latter event being by them more desired than such a horrible existence as was accorded them. Passing along a roadway, inside the castle walls, you see what work has been done here. The road has been cut through solid rocks and made level and smooth as the finest boulevard. The masonry that has been constructed on either side has been unchanged for centuries, save that the ivy creeps all over it. Soon a delightful path is pursued amid stately cedars, like those of Lebanon. At length you come to a widely extended lawn, dotted here and there with beds of flowers, and skirting this, the waters of the Avon glide. You forget that you are inside the walls of a feudal castle as you walk still farther and come to a lovely lake on whose waters the swan convoys his family, like a proud ship leading a little fleet. You turn to the right and enter a structure in which is kept a great marble vase, one of the treasures of the Earl of Warwick, the wonderful proportions of which, an Englishman, who looks nearly as old as the vase itself, begins in a monotonous voice to explain to you. The old man has his speech well in hand, and his voice rises and falls in uniform degrees for a little while, until at last it reaches a pitch from which he does not seem willing that it should descend, and he continues there to point out the vines and clusters and other carvings on the great object of his reverence. He has told his story so often that he knows just where to pause, and there is a mathematical regularity in his intonations that once heard will never be forgotten. If I were to revisit the castle, I certainly would not care to see the vase again, but I would desire to hear the squeaking old voice of the little interpreter, and am inclined to believe that he will live longer than he otherwise would, because he thinks no one could do justice to the earl's treasure if he were to die. The present Earl of Warwick lives in the castle, or a part of it large enough to accommodate a hundred families. A large part of that which he occupies is opened to public inspection at all times, save when he is entertaining.

Royalty and nobility live in constant fear of dynamite, hence the premises are well guarded. Old and reliable soldiers who have had experience in the detective service are employed. You are courteously shown through dining-rooms and bed-chambers and halls and parlors, where you may see elaborately framed pictures, painted by the old masters. There is seemingly no end of tables, secretaries, and escritoires, richly inlaid and curiously wrought. Mosaics of delicate workmanship, and tapestries fashioned with exquisite skill, excite your wonder and call forth your admiration. I have often seen displays of modern splendor, but in my wildest dreams I never pictured such treasures as are possessed by the Earl of Warwick.

And yet I have asked myself if there is not a certain sort of vulgarity in making these displays of the possessions of a family to strangers, and that for a shilling a person. The castle, except on great occasions, is only a museum, and not in any true sense a home. Imagine, if you can, some wealthy and cultured American citizen inviting the world to come and look through his parlors and bed-chambers and halls, at twenty-five cents a visit. I presume many of us would go to look, but it would be without much reverence for the proprietor. There is something here to interest all varieties of taste. One who is weary of paintings and furniture and statuary, may probably be amused by a visit to the side-board, and an inspection of the china. Those who have more delight in the rigid features of the Warwick history, can examine the old armor or try on the iron helmet, or take both hands and lift the rude sword, or gaze into the depths of the mush-pot of the giant of Warwick. What a hard head and stiff neck, what strong muscles and wonderful digestive powers the old fellow must have had !

Kenilworth Castle, but a few miles distant, is a complete ruin. No one can visit it without being impressed with the magnificence that once reigned there. Sir Walter Scott has immortalized it. In the marks of time on its crumbling walls and desolate dungeons and bold towers, we may learn something of belittled greatness and fading glory. God alone is great. The stone pillars that supported the floor of the banquet hall are standing, but every particle of the floor is gone. The revelers have been sleeping for centuries. There is a poetic beauty in these old ruins. A hundred school children, off for a holiday, were climbing over the walls, peering into the dungeons, or rollicking on the grass. A young couple had sought out a quiet place in a half-perished doorway, to play over again the old scene between " Leicester " and the " Queen," when the faithless husband whispered words of love in the not unwilling ears of his gracious sovereign. A boy, who may have been the direct descendant of Scott's " Flibbertigibbet," was turning handsprings where once royalty was entertained. A flock of sheep, some of whose ancestry may have been slaughtered by the earl on the famous visit of Elizabeth to his castle, were nipping the grass, all unconscious of the dignity of their grazing on such hallowed soil. The expenditure of three million dollars had not been enough to keep the castle in repair. Its gates are guarded now simply to secure sixpence from the tourist. The great festival held here in honor of Queen Elizabeth, in 1475, and so graphically pictured by Scott in his half-historic novel, marked the greatest day of the glory of Kenilworth Castle. In no place is the ivy more beautiful, as it creeps over the crumbling walls, and, like a gentle friend, seeks to shield them from vulgar gaze. It is nature's mantle of charity, concealing, and even beautifying, what it can not restore.

CHAPTER IV.

THE London papers were filled with accounts of the cholera in Russia, and there was little doubt that it was moving westward. If we remained long in England it would not be prudent to cross the North Sea. We therefore hastily determined on our future course, and started out toward the dreaded disease, with the purpose of visiting parts of Germany and getting away before the cholera put in its appearance. Experienced travelers laughed and shook their heads significantly as we spoke of going by Harwich to Rotterdam. I learned in a few hours the cause of their significant looks. It was ten o'clock at night when we stepped on board the little steamer at Harwich. The luxury of a night's sleep, after the fatigue of the day, was soon to be realized, and at once we repaired to our state-room, for which we had telegraphed from London. The state-room was a little larger than four steamer trunks. It was higher and wider than the pile of trunks would be if economically packed.

Within this, four of us were stowed away like sardines
in a box. I was soon asleep from sheer weariness, but
found it convenient to get awake. The boat reminded
me of a nervous child. The mother dreads to see it
begin to move. It foretells a time of tossing and
tempest. The child stirred! Such a restless boat I
never had traveled on. It got on one side for a second
or two, and you adjusted yourself to this, in the belief
that by lying at the proper angle you could surely
sleep, but quick as a flash it dispelled the vain hope.
It turned on the other side, and you turned with it.
Then it tossed off the watery spread and sat up. It
stood upright. It fell down and got up. It waltzed
over the waves until it grew dizzy, and sat down with
you again. It danced like a barefooted boy that has
unintentionally stepped on a wasp's nest, or has found
the injudiciousness of interfering with a bumble-bee
when it is gathering sweetness from a red clover blos-
som. The waters ran over the deck and swished up
against the port windows. Then one-fourth of our
state-room began to groan. It was something like the
groan of Ajax when Æneas began breaking off bushes
with which to cover the altar, and found out that in
place of sap flowing therefrom, it was blood that came
from the body of Ajax, and the bush was the growth
of a spear that had pierced his body. I do not recall
the Latin accurately, but remember the Irishman's

account of the fright of the rash man who pulled away the branch when he saw the blood:

"My hair stood on end, and my voice stuck in my throat, and niver a word could I say at all."

The groan was not an English one. The gentleman is a professor in a school where foreign languages are taught. It was a groan unlike anything I had ever heard before. It was followed by another and then another. I thought the fellow must be dying, and stirred up the doctor. The doctor was sound asleep and was hard to waken, but I wakened him. I did not propose to be tossed about in that rough sea and listen to that unearthly groaning all by myself. It was too lonesome. I wanted company. The professor was not a total abstainer. He believed that he ought to take brandy for his stomach's sake, and he took it. But his stomach did not propose to yield the struggle to anything so weak. The battle lasted till daylight, and I had to lie there and listen to it with that peculiarly soothed nervous feeling in the epigastric regions that a companion's sea-sickness always produces. But the doctor did not get asleep again. Though I could not see him, there was consolation in the fact that he was wide awake. He got up and went on deck. When he came below again, he reported three hundred sick! I warned him of the dangers of exaggeration. He repeated his assertion. I told him there were only two hundred and fifty aboard, and I knew one who was not sick. He replied that he was that happy individual. I thought it was I.

"But how did you make out three hundred when there are only two hundred and fifty aboard?"

"Several of them are sick enough to count twice," he replied.

And the professor thought we were talking of him.

We had scarcely left Rotterdam when we had our first experience of the difficulties attending travel in a country of whose speech we were wholly ignorant. A gentleman from Chicago and his accomplished wife, who were taking a tour of Europe, were on the tram with us. The gentleman's countenance betokened perplexity. His wife seemed to take in the ridiculous side of the affair as well as the serious. There was something wrong with the tickets, which the conductor insisted on explaining in Dutch. The gentleman answered in the purest Anglo-Saxon. The conductor did not understand the passenger, and the passenger did not understand the conductor. The conductor thought the passenger was stupid, and the passenger was sure the conductor was dumb. An appeal to the German language was useless, for the Hollander knew as little of that as he did of English. The way to end a dispute of this kind is always to put your hand in your pocket and hold out enough money. If the coin you offer is large enough to talk, the explanation is soon made by the simple transfer of the money to your neighbor's pocket.

It was under these circumstances we met Mr. and Mrs. Case, and we had occasion to be profited by the acquaintance many days afterward.

I deeply regret that we left the Hotel Des Indes without getting a photograph of the head porter. He is a little over five feet in height, and is built as square as a stick of stovewood. He stood at the doorway, on the arrival of the carriage, dressed in a suit of sky-blue. His cap was of the same color, and, besides the name of the hotel, had on it several bands of gold lace. About the sleeves of his coat were three bands somewhat wider than those on his cap. The moment his eyes met ours he lifted his right hand to his cap, extended his arm at right angles to his body, held the arm in that position several seconds, and then let the hand come to his side with as much fixedness of motion as a pump handle has when being lowered to the stock. He was as sober as a grave-yard. His person did not bend in the least. He was the personification of porterial dignity. He quietly ordered the subordinates to their duty, and in broken English assured us that we were welcome guests at the hotel. When we approached him for information, or gave him a few pfennigs, he always saluted us with the same stately dignity. I felt somewhat awed in his presence, and wondered if he were not a relative of the little Queen of Holland, but the doctor assured me that he was only the porter, and I was comfortable.

We got on the top of the tram car and rode out to Scheveningen, a sea-side resort, three miles distant. The trip to this watering-place is one never to be forgotten. It takes you under the leafy boughs of forest trees that grow so thickly above you that you seldom get a glimpse of the sun. The car goes so near the trees that you may reach over and touch their trunks, while the branches are cut away above so as to leave but a few inches between them and your hat. You may look down this fair bower for two miles and see it grow narrower at the further end. It is straight as an arrow, and is not equaled anywhere in Europe. This at least is the testimony of those who have traveled most widely. The peasantry wear wooden shoes, and old men and women walk along the streets leaning on staves, and wearing shoes whose dull thuds betoken the absence of all elasticity. Young men and women walk gaily along with the firm and resolute rapping of wooden heels on the sidewalk, while the clatter of the little children's shoes sounds merrily, and tells of poverty and contentment.

Passing over a gracefully sloping hill, there is presented a picture that must awaken interest. Here

surge the waters of the North Sea. More than a
thousand people are gathered together on the sand.
Temporary tents are erected, in which all sorts of
trinkets are sold. Half the multitude are sitting in
little willow chairs that have a grotesque appearance.
If you will make a large clothes-basket, with one end
square, in place of oval, and in this end have a willow
seat, so that you might sit in it when the basket is on
the square end, you have a model of these resting
places of the Hollanders by the sea-shore. They are
comfortable and light, and may be readily turned in
any desired direction. They did not seem to be well
fitted for lovers, since they accommodate but one person. But it is easy to join them together, and the heart
may be won by the flash of the eye, and possibly by
low-spoken Hollandish words. My impression, however, was shown to be false, as a young lady, who
was familiar with the habits of the people, said that
there was plenty of room in one of these little sitting-
baskets for two persons, if they were sufficiently
attracted to one another. The pleasure seekers seemed
to be enjoying their leisure hours in a rational way.
Ladies were reading, sleeping, conversing, knitting, or
working embroidery, while the little children were
digging in the sand about them.

We wanted to go in bathing, and had some difficulty
in finding the proper place to hire suits, and then the

right way to get into these suits. We finally entered a large wagon, which was really a cottage on wheels, where we prepared ourselves for the sea. A sturdy old man dragged the wagon down into the water, and when you opened the door of your little apartment you stepped into the water about your knees. There is no satisfaction in bathing where one has to lie down to get the surf washed over him. We went out and fought waves breast high. The wagoner came wading out, and by violent gestures warned us to go no further. It was rather hard to obey; but, supposing that he knew more about this than we did, and not knowing how to deal with Dutch waters in case of danger, we came to him. He pointed to his breast, and there was a gold medal, given him by the government, for saving twenty people from drowning. I did not fully understand him, but supposed he said that they were venturesome fools, like some other people he had to deal with. Why he did not encourage us to go out farther, and get another medal, I can not tell. Some people are lacking in the spirit of enterprise. But it was a singular spectacle—the honest old barefooted man, with his wet clothes all in tatters, and yet about his neck a gold medal of great value. We had no medals on hand, so we gave him twenty pfennigs (four cents) for his kindness to our families in saving our lives. A horse fair is held at Scheveningen,

4

which the little girl Queen, eleven years old, was
to grace on the morrow by her presence. But as
we had seen queenly little girls forty years ago, we
had no desire to see a child who was to be used as an
advertisement for a horse fair!

After buying a pair of wooden shoes for myself,
which nearly half filled the doctor's box, we returned
to The Hague. A pleasant evening drive about the
city, and a vain search for the grave of Barneveldt,
closed up the exercises for the evening. In the morning we visited the Royal Museum, and were delighted
with the splendid exhibition of pictures. The fame
of " Paul Potter's Bull " is well merited, and is not to
be judged by the so-called copies that are to be found
in so many places. But it is train time, and so bidding
our friends adieu, and tipping a half-dozen people at
the hotel, and acknowledging the profound salute of
the porter, we arrived at the depot, only to find out
that we had tickets by another road, and that our
train did not go until in the afternoon. We returned
to the city, and called on the United States minister.
He lives in seclusion, not speaking the language, and
having no household to share his perplexities and
entertain his visitors. We assured him that we did
not want to borrow money, which, when he heard, he
expressed himself willing to loan us. We did not
want to be shown about the city, or presented to the

little Queen. He breathed a sigh of relief at that, but would have been delighted to take us everywhere and tell us everything. We had been paying so many people in the city for services not needed, that we felt it would be out of place not to give him something too, and so we had called to pay him our respects. He had lived so long among these solemn Hollanders, that he had forgotten how to laugh, but, in order to be respectful, forced himself to smile.

We went back to the hotel, and received the same formal, soldierly salute from the porter that we had on our first arrival. It was somewhat of a recompense for the disappointment we had experienced. As we strolled about under the lime trees, we met Mrs. Case, who, while her husband busied himself with the barber, had started out with her kodak to catch a few pictures. I detected in the smile she gave us something more mischievous than a recognition. It meant, in plain Chicago words, which she was too polite to use: "Gentlemen, you got left!" We joined her in the artist's walk, and came on that island described by Motley as: "Fringed with weeping willows and tufted all over with lilacs, laburnums, and other shrubs, in the center of a miniature lake." Now, as on the morning when Barneveldt was executed, "the white swans were sailing to and fro over the silver basin." We knew something more of the situation than before, and after seeing that the lake was duly kodaked, went to the court-yard where Barneveldt was executed. No wonder that residents of The Hague do not care to point strangers to that spot where the cruelty and injustice of Maurice disgraced the noble House of Orange, and left on his own name the stain of a patriot's blood. Here, on that bright May morning, 1619, sat the rude soldiers casting dice as to the destiny of the soul of Barneveldt. On these walls were displayed caricatures of the noblest statesman of Holland. I can almost see the old Advocate, more than seventy years of age, walking out on the scaffold, as he leans heavily on his staff, and looks with wonder over the three thousand ignorant people who believed him guilty of treason to the state. Here is the very spot where his voice, broken with sorrow and disappointment, yet sweet as the words of the martyr, is heard: "This, then, is the reward of forty years' service to the state!" There, where my friend is pointing her kodak, is the spot where he kneels with his face toward his house, and, while the executioner draws his sword, bends over the sand that is to drink in his blood, saying with a firm voice:

"Christ shall be my guide. O Lord! my Heavenly Father, receive my spirit."

It is proper also to record the fact that the wife of the Advocate never petitioned for her husband's pardon, because she knew he had committed no offense, and to have sued for pardon would have been the admission of a crime. A tablet in the wall of the court-yard records the fact of his death. Blessings come to us in the guise of disappointments. I was glad that we did not get off on the morning train. We had an opportunity of formally bidding the head porter another farewell, slipping a small coin into his hands, and the grave old man was just bringing down his hand to his side, as he had done in the morning, when our carriage turned the corner. Holland has been rescued from the sea, and might easily be given back to its dominion again. In fact this was done when the brave people warred against Spain. The country is very fertile, and in many parts the waters of the canals are kept pure by wind-mills, which pump it out to higher levels.

CHAPTER V.

S we travel southward, toward Cologne, we find it convenient to select compartments where smoking is not permitted. Here I take my first lesson in Dutch. On the doors of certain compartments you will see the words, "Niet Rooken." The interpretation of this is, "No smoking permitted." Just here I must say that the most selfish habit on earth is that of the smoker. He gets to windward of you, and, no matter how mean the quality of his cigar or pipe, whiffs away, with the smoke blowing in your face. He is seldom polite enough to ask if the use of tobacco is unpleasant to you. He does not care. But, of all places in the world, tobacco smoke in Holland is the vilest. The smoker will even come into the compartment where smoking is forbidden, and fumigate you until you attract his attention and point to the "Niet Rooken" on the wall, and then he casts a look of contempt at you, accompanied by a dismal grunt, that shows in what estimation you are held. It is more than possible that someone may read this page with a cigar between his lips, who will stop just here to shake off the ashes, and give a similar utterance to his feelings, suggesting that such delicate people had better stay at home. But in the fact that he is too far away for me either to be stifled with the smoke or hear the criticism, I find consolation. There is no stop made for dinner. There is no opportunity to get refreshments, unless you rush from the car and are back again in three minutes. Beer is peddled along in glasses, and is purchased by passengers, who give up the glasses at the next stop that is made. The compartment was crowded. We discussed freely the condition of Europe, and especially the lack of ordinary comforts on the railways. We were hungry, and there is a sort of traditionary belief that when men are hungry they are not amiable. Two English ladies proposed to give us a regular tea-party. We gladly accepted, and a traveling basket was drawn from under the seat. The contents of that basket were a revelation. A jar of water was produced. A bright little tea-kettle followed. A lamp was lighted, and in a few minutes the kettle was boiled, and, with spoons and knives and forks and sugar and sandwiches, we had a refined little tea-party. The doctor's soul seemed to revive with the luxurious living. He repeated poetry and talked so much philosophy that I became alarmed for his safety. Tea is the true stimulus. The dish-washing,

under the circumstances, was rather embarrassing.
My idea, that the cup must be washed without touching it with your hands, could not well be executed,
and there was a lively discussion as to which one of
the party was the most skillful. The ladies had been
benefactresses. They had fed the hungry. But, as it
proved some days afterward, they had also been casting bread on the waters, for the doctor's medical counsel was sought and freely given in the serious sickness
of one of them. As for myself I had no way of
expressing my gratitude except by the heartiness with
which I partook of the novel repast.

We experienced on this trip the annoyances of the
continental custom-house. One must take all his luggage from the compartment into the custom-room,
to be examined, and then skirmish about in search
of his box, and, having found it, open it and his
satchel, and endure the agony of seeing sacred apparel
handled by officious officials. Then he fees a porter
to take back the box to the train, and attempts to pass
out. A guard prevents him, and points to another
room through which he must go. This room is simply a beer hall. The door from it to the platform is
locked, and he must remain there fully fifteen minutes, breathing a foul air that is doubly polluted with
the fumes of tobacco and the stench of fermented
liquors, before he can return to his car. Some

Americans fall in with the custom of the country, and spend the time drinking beer. Others use rather inelegant, but strongly expressive, adjectives; while a few, like myself, give themselves to quiet meditation, on the comforts of home and the glory of American citizenship.

The cathedral at Cologne is the most impressive structure of the kind in Europe. Its proportions are on a scale that surprise us, though we had been expecting something marvelous. It is four hundred and fifty feet long, two hundred and one feet wide, and one of its towers is five hundred and eleven feet high. There is nothing that approaches it in the fairness of its proportions. The parts seem to be in perfect harmony with each other. In 1795 the French used this magnificent structure to store away hay in. It is a long road that has no turnings in it. In 1870 the Germans had their revenge, if the word can be at all used in regard to a house of worship. Remembering the insults that had been heaped on them by the French, seventy-five years before, they made a bell for their cathedral, weighing twenty-five tons, out of cannon captured from the French. Every time the bell rings they may recall their hatred and their triumph. Much of this building is used for shrines and statues and confessionals. The stained-glass windows represent Bible incidents, particularly those in

which the Virgin figured.   Long after the special
services were over, occasional worshipers lingered on
their knees, with troubled faces, looking with tear-
dimmed eyes at the picture or statue of some favorite
saint.   Under a slab in the pavement lies the heart
of Marie de Medici.   The work of construction was
carried on through several centuries, and besides the
gifts of the rich and poor, vast sums were added
through the profits of lotteries.   The slowness of the
work of construction could fairly be attributed to the
vastness of the undertaking, but some zealous devotees
attributed it to the devil, who became jealous and
vowed that it should never be completed.   But the
means resorted to would seem to indicate that, either
the devil was not jealous or else that his kingdom
must have been divided against itself, as the lottery
is under his special protection.

What magnificent temples ignorance is willing to
build to that very power by which it is enslaved !
The cathedral at Cologne has been erected by the
contributions of kings, and by the sacrifices of the
poor and needy.   But it is a law everywhere prev-
alent, that the more we sacrifice in behalf of any
cause, the dearer it becomes to us, and that where we
give but little we love but little.   The protestant
world has much to learn, not in the way of erecting
costly material structures, but in enlarged offerings to

the cause of Christian evangelization and consequent freedom.

As there was but little of interest on the Rhine, between Cologne and Bonn, we determined to go by rail to the latter place and take the steamer there to Mayence. This arrangement enabled us to sleep as long as we desired in the morning, and have ample time to overtake the boat on the river. The tourist who makes his first trip will be annoyed and confused with the number of persons to whom he must give money for services. He does not know very well how little he is giving, and he is equally in ignorance of the number of hands that will be reached out to him. This was specially manifest on our Rhine trip. The fees exacted are small; so were the flies in Egypt, but they were unnumbered. Arriving at Bonn, we hired an expressman to take our luggage across to the boat, while we sauntered leisurely along the pleasant walk between the station and the boat landing. When we arrived at the landing, we found our boxes at the farther side of the street from the boat. The porter of the boat could not cross the street for the boxes. The porter on the street dare not carry them on the boat. The street porter had to be feed for taking them across the street. The expressman dare not leave them on the side next the river. The boat porter was paid for carrying them to the boat. The baggageman on the boat was paid for putting a tab on them that marked their destination. At Mayence the boat porter was again feed for carrying them to the hack. The hackman received his usual tip, and at the hotel the porter was paid for taking them to our room. The amount necessarily paid was very little, and one felt his importance in having so many hired servants to do his bidding. Americans generally give five times too much, and, of course, no change is returned. We are, however, rapidly adopting this pernicious habit at home, and in some places where men are supposed to be hired by wealthy corporations, they actually pay something for the privilege of doing the work. No one begrudges the poor fellows the little they receive, but it is annoying to be compelled to hire all the servants at a hotel where you have paid your bills in full. The only one in Europe who refused an offered gratuity, was a lady clerk in Paris, who courteously handed back the coin, saying:

"I have resolved to make my employer pay my salary, and then I can be courteous without sacrificing my dignity. I hope you will not think me impolite, but what I have done has been without hope of reward." ·

The ten hours' ride on the Rhine from Bonn to Mayence is full of interest. The river runs between two mountain regions and the valley is so narrow that the hills on both sides of the river rising several hundred feet above you, are seen in all the minute details of rock, ravine, and vineyards. Rugged as these mountains are, the enterprising Germans have discovered that, by making terraces on their sides, little vineyards may be cultivated. These terraced plots vary in size from a few feet to several acres. The stone walls that keep in the soil so that it may not be washed down the mountain sides, have been the work of centuries. The soil itself has been carried up from the banks of the river on the heads of toilers, many of whom were women.

These little vineyards have no uniformity in shape or size, and the divisions between them are distinctly marked. A wall, forty feet in height, may have been built to support a space of half an acre, and next to it a wall, ten feet high, to form the outer foundation for a dozen vines. This variety of size and shape gives to the mountain sides a peculiar charm. But that which awakens the deepest interest is the ruins of the old castles, which must have flourished as early as the twelfth century. They are on the tops of mountainous bluffs which, seen from the river, appear almost inaccessible. How the stones were ever carried to such heights is a mystery to us. These ruins are eloquent lessons that tell of unrequited toil, suffering, ambition, blighted fortunes, and vanished hopes. Legends,

that may be more than half historic, still exist. They
tell the old story of love and jealousy, and disappointment and crime. Some of these legends are full of
pathos and have been the models for modern novelists.
A single illustration will be sufficient to show how full
of the poetry of tenderness some of them are. On the
summit of Drachenfel's Mountain, which is nine hundred and ten feet high, are the ruins of Drachenfel's
Castle, built in the twelfth century. Roland, a young
nephew of Charlemagne, came to the castle. He did
not come as a lover, for he knew nothing of the inhabitants of it. The knight who then owned the castle
received the young man favorably and urged him to
remain with him. The youth, pleased with the entertainment, consented. So favorably did Roland impress
his host, that he brought his daughter to the table,
where she was formally presented to the young and
gifted Roland. It was the old story of love at first
sight. In all his life Roland had never seen one
whose beauty and grace so filled his soul. The
maiden, whose name was Hildegunde, was an only
daughter, the pride of her father's life. Fill in, as
you choose, the hours of their courtship, the under-
standings and misunderstandings. Nothing is new in
love, and nothing strange in it, and nothing false.
Anything you may desire to say has been said a thousand times. After all their meetings and partings,

the "pledge was snatched from her finger feignedly
resisting." And when the pledge is once secured it is
an easy matter to get possession of the heart. Roland
and Hildegunde, on Drachenfels, were as near heaven
as it is permitted mortals to be. A new castle was
planned. Then came a message from Charlemagne
ordering Roland to hasten to Spain and lead a host
against the Saracens. The plans of the lovers were
disconcerted. As a true knight he dare not hesitate,
and yet, Hildegunde believed that Roland would never
return. She did not doubt his loyalty and devotion
to her. She saw in her dreams the hero of the war,
her lover, surrounded by the cruel Saracens, who
fought like demons, and when Roland could no longer
maintain himself against the fearful odds, he fell, with
his face to the foe, gasping even in death the name of
Hildegunde. The presentiment of the lady, that had
taken such definite form, at last was realized to her.
Roland was wounded, and soon after the tidings came
that he was dead. Her father saw and shared her
grief, not only because of sympathy with his daughter
but because of his attachment to the noble youth who
was to claim her hand. Hildegunde, believing that
her lover was dead, determined that she, too, would
die even a more cruel death. She would die to the
world in the gloom of the cloister. A few months
after she had left her father's castle, a distinguished

visitor arrived and was ushered into the presence of Heribert, the father of Hildegunde. Heribert first uttered a cry of joy, but instantly bowed his head, covering his face with his hands. To Roland's eager inquiries for Hildegunde, he at last said, with a hoarse voice, "She is now the Bride of Heaven." Roland, stricken dumb, left the castle. He at once began the erection of a castle, Rolandseck. This overlooked the convent, and he hoped that sometimes, from it, he might see Hildegunde, as she went from the little chapel. He saw her daily, but she gave him no token of recognition. One morning she did not appear, and the day following he saw the sad procession bearing forth her body for sepulture. She was now twice dead to him, and his mind wandered as well as his body. Soon after, he was found cold in death, but his glazed eye was turned toward the spot where he had last seen his beloved Hildegunde.

This is substantially the story as it will be told, allowing for the license which I have taken with a legend. But one great lesson the story teaches, even if the tale itself be without foundation in fact, and that is the hateful system of both old and new Rome, that teaches its deluded votaries that such cruel sacrifices are pleasing to Him who came to brighten and beautify life, and who ordained that true love is never to be laid on any altar of sacrifice.

The boat was crowded with tourists. We ordered our meals on the forward deck, and looked out with wonder and delight at mountains, to whose very summits the vines were growing. The day was perfect, and the sunlight and shadows recalled the legends of the Rhine.

I looked out dreamily over the scene that, for nine hours, had been observed with animation. I began to philosophize, for a hundred passengers were drinking Rhenish wine from these very vineyards. I wondered if our civilization was very far superior to that of seven centuries ago. The castles are in ruins, but the mountain sides are clothed with vines, the product of which destroys the peace and puts out the light in ten thousand homes.

One of these old castles is owned by an American, and as we came opposite to it, we felt a thrill of patriotism, for from the turret floated the American flag. "The stars and stripes!" cried someone in a fit of enthusiasm, and then several hundred Americans sent up a cheer, that told of devotion to a land that was as dear to us as "Fatherland" could possibly be to the Germans.

The channel at Bingen is so nearly obstructed by rocks, that it requires skillful piloting to get through, and the attempt is never made in foggy weather. But the town of Bingen called up the sweet little poem of

5

Caroline Norton, " Bingen on the Rhine," where the
dying soldier in Algiers tells his comrade of his birthplace and mother and sister, and of "another—not a
sister," whom he had known in the happy days gone
by.

> "I saw the blue Rhine sweep along — I heard, or
>   seemed to hear,
> The German songs we used to sing, in chorus
>   sweet and clear,
> And down the pleasant river, and up the slanting
>   hill,
> The echoing chorus sounded through the evening
>   calm and still;
> And her glad blue eyes were on me, as we passed
>   with friendly talk
> Down many a path beloved of yore, and well-
>   remembered walk,
> And her little hand lay lightly, confidingly in mine;
> But we'll meet no more at Bingen — loved Bingen
>   on the Rhine."

CHAPTER VI.

E arrived at Mayence too late for the train to Heidelberg, and concluded to remain over Sabbath. There was no English services of any sort, and so we quietly rested at our hotel. We are really in a fortified city. A great fortress is above us, and every hill is fortified. Twelve thousand soldiers are out maneuvering, and parading the streets. For every soldier in the army, there is at least one woman gathering in the harvest. Europe pays for her military glory. I was not sorry to see the rain come on in such quantity as to stop the meaningless parade. The servants ran into the room to see that the windows were closed. Vivid lightning flashed through the air, and the peals of thunder were enough to make one who believed that noise was dangerous, tremble. The doctor wanted to know whether this storm was more violent than others. Notwithstanding the violence of the storm, I could not restrain some show of merriment when he asked about the " *dunner und blitz.*" The words seemed, however, far more

(67)

expressive than our common thunder and lightning.
But the quality of the German thunder and lightning
demanded stronger words than we usually employ in
this country. Some people think that they have fallen
in hard lines when they must go to church. I confess that the hardest part of my experience was, that
I could not go to church. Possibly, if I had the opportunity, I might not prize it so highly.

There were two things in Heidelberg to attract us
thither—the castle and the university. The former
fully came up to our expectations. Heidelberg is an
important point, on account of its position, being situated at the junction of the Neckar with the Rhine.

The city, of about fifteen thousand, lies in the
valley at the foot of the Königstuhl, on the one
side, and of the Heiligenberg, on the other. The
mountain on which the castle is situated may be
ascended either by a cog-wheel railroad or by carriages. We went by the inclined road to the top of
the mountain, and as we went up, speculated on the
possibility of a rapid descent. The view from the summit is exceptionally fine. Beneath you, lies the city,
appearing very little (as most things and people
do), when looked down on. The valleys of the Rhine
and Neckar, with the now distant vine-clad mountains,
are seen at a single glance, but give you life-long and
pleasing remembrances. The usual beer garden is on

the summit, and two hundred visitors were seated among the trees, looking down on the city, that nestles about the base of the mountain. Half way down the mountain, are the ruins of the castle, which are the most extensive to be seen in Europe. The structure has had a remarkable history. It was begun in the thirteenth century, and for two hundred years the work of extending and strengthening it went on. It was, however, blown up by the French in 1689, wholly dismantled in 1693, and, as if to complete its ruin, was struck by lightning in 1764. But, notwithstanding all these things, its ruins are on a scale that is simply magnificent. In a state of comparative preservation, you may see relics of the work of old masters, specimens of sculpture, in bas-reliefs and statues, approaching the perfect, and these, on walls that seem ready to fall. The guide whom we employed was an intelligent man, but full of hatred to the French. He took delight in expatiating on the vandalism of an army, that had no reverence for works of art. I pointed out the dark, cruel dungeons of the castle, and asked him what he thought of a people that would shut human beings in such places as these.

As we returned to the city, we met some forty of the students of the university. I can have some little respect for the Indians, who disfigure and deform their bodies, for they are savages; but for these young men, who glory in their scars, gotten in duels, I have nothing but pity and contempt. The duel has become an established thing now at Heidelberg. The young man who enters one of the fraternities, is expected to fight with some student of the other fraternity, and the one who gets the ugliest scars, is the hero of the school. We had an opportunity to witness two of these silly combats, falsely called duels, but declined. One of our companions waited to see the fight, and to him I am indebted for a full description. The young men have their throats guarded, so that they may escape death. They stand close together, so that they can not cut each other with the points of their swords. Two seconds rest on their knees between them, and with swords, guard the throats of the principals, who cut and slash, with but little skill, at each other's brows and cheeks. A surgeon stands by, and every few minutes the fight is stopped, that he may examine the cuts, to see whether they are sufficiently deep to make ugly scars. Meantime, the fighters wipe the blood from their swords, and if the surgeon is not satisfied that they will appear sufficiently disfigured, he orders them to fight again. When it is over, the young man with his scarred face, receives an ovation from his friends, and is ever afterward proud of the number of scars he bears. It seems incredible to us, that this should be so; but some of the men we saw, had on their brows and cheeks, as many as twenty scars, that showed but little care for neat healing. The elegant apparel worn by these students, only sets off, in a more repulsive light, the ugliness of their faces. Such is the boasted civilization of the great university of Germany. In all my life I have seen nothing so repulsive. If they had fought to kill, it could not have been worse. As it is, the university duelist is as cowardly as he is brutal. Scars gotten in defense of the truth, are not dishonorable. The patriot may bear them as a distinction of true worth. But a scar that is gotten in such a silly and disgusting manner, would be, in America, a badge of dishonor, to be carried about with shame and humility. If some enterprising German were to bring a couple of dozen of these students to our country for exhibition, they would awaken as much curiosity as the "Wild West Show" does in London or Paris. The facts given, appear all the more incredible, because of the gentlemanly bearing of the young men.

The great tun is in the vaults of the castle. It discounts all the beer kegs that have ever been made. It was constructed in the vaults, and has never been moved from its position. As it lies on its side it measures thirty-two feet in length, and twenty-six feet in height. It has a capacity of 50,000 gallons. It has been filled and emptied three times. If some

old toper had been drinking from it, it would make
him thirsty to look at ordinary whisky barrels afterward.   Some idiot conceived the idea of building a-
platform on it for a dancing hall.   It is just the size
of a section, taken through the center of the tun, and
is therefore twenty-six by thirty-two feet.   A rough
stairway leads up to this platform, and everything
about the tun and the vaults is as rough as the stairs.

From Heidelberg to Munich is a trip of which I
can write but little, as we made it by night.   One
finds quite as much comfort, and far less expense,
traveling in Europe, on a second, or even third-class
ticket, than on a first.   Sleeping cars are but little
used, especially in the British Isles, where the distance to be traveled is short.   But we wanted to go
to Munich by a sleeper.   It was nearly train time, and
we had no sleeping-car ticket.   So we walked along
the platform saying, "schlafen zug!" to every railroad
guard or other official we met.   No one heeded our
cry, but we knew that we were right, so we kept on,
the doctor walking on one side of the platform and I
on the other, and each one of us saying, eagerly,
"München schlafen zug !"   At last we found a guard,
or conductor, who opened a door, and bade us enter.
We were prisoners, securely locked within a finely
upholstered compartment.   No porter came to the
door, when we wanted to retire, to make up our

berths. To all appearance we were only in a well-
gotten-up day car, with a wash-room attached. The
doctor insisted that, somehow or other, it must be a
sleeping car, for both of us had asked for a "schlafen
zug." He is a curious sort of fellow, and began at
last, like a spoiled child, to pull at all the straps and
buttons about the car. I assured him that it was a
sleeper, but that the Germans sat up while they slept.
I had often seen others do this. "You mean at our
church," the doctor said. There was somewhat of
malice in the speech, and I thought he might go on
and wear himself out strap-pulling. It would make
him more reasonable. After some ten minutes of
diligent work, he pulled the right strap, and out shot
the seat, and down came the back, and up sprang a
pillow. A similar pull at a strap on the other side of
the compartment was made, and a splendid bed, for
one person, was ready for occupancy. I looked out of
the window, while my companion stretched himself
out on the soft bed, saying, with an air of triumph,
"I told you!" "It took you a long time to find it
out. Why didn't you ask me about it, and save all
your trouble?" But I soon followed his example,
and we, like two innocent children, fell asleep, locked
in our compartment, and dreamed of friends thousands of miles away. How long our slumbers lasted
I could not tell; but as the day began to break, the

conductor opened the door, and demanded our tickets. He then held the door open, and seemed to want something else, but to be too modest to ask for it. Supposing it to be money, but not knowing whether he wanted forty francs for the car, or a milder tip for himself, I gave him a large tip, amounting to five francs. He opened his eyes and shut the door. I am afraid that he did not give the railroad a commission out of his gratuity. We saw no one else to give money to, and quietly slept until time for preparations for leaving the train. It was quite amusing to see the doctor washing his hands and face in a sleeper in which there were no towels. He got along very well with the matter until he came to dry his face without a towel. It reminded me of a bird shaking its wings after the morning's ablution. Arrived at the station, we were courteously invited to get out. We obeyed. The night's rest had cost us half a dollar each, and we could not find anyone willing to take the remaining francs. But I presume, that had it not been for the doctor's persistence, in investigating, we would both have sat up till morning, and voted the "schlafen zug" a failure.

The royal palace at Munich surprised us by its grandeur. We were conducted through halls, chambers, reception-rooms, state-rooms, and galleries, where splendid paintings, in frames of gorgeous patterns, seemed to strive in rivalry with tapestries and inlaid furniture, most richly carved. Mosaics, so delicate in their construction that you had to inspect them closely to confirm your faith that they were what they purported to be. A few of the names given to the different rooms of the palace are suggestive, as the ball-room, the card-rooms, the Battle Salôn, the Hall of Charlemagne, the Barbarossa Hall, the Hapsburg Saloon, and the Throne Room. The guard, who conducted us through the palace, spoke only in German. It would be an insult to explain the garnishing of the palace and its furnishing in any tongue, save German. Yet, his articulation was very distinct, and he spoke slowly and in a sort of reverential tone, not unlike what some people employ when leading in formal prayers. He wanted to linger in the hall where are the portraits of thirty-six beautiful women. They must have been pretty, or they surely would not have been thus distinguished; but I failed to see the exceeding comeliness of form and feature that entitled them to be thus singled out from among their sisters. You can find thirty-six handsomer ladies in any good-sized college town, who have not stood before the marriage altar, and are, like Queen Elizabeth, " In maiden meditation, fancy free." But the proper thing to do is, go along with the crowd and look appreciatively, and listen carefully, no matter whether you comprehend what is said or not.

When we arrived at the Old Pinakothek or Gallery of Ancient Masters, we found it closed; but a few gentle raps at the door brought the keeper, who assured us that it was not possible for us to be admitted. We gave the venerable lady a little silver for treating us so kindly, and she held out her hand for more. We gave it. Then she opened the door and turned us loose at pleasure to revel among the works of the old artists. It was the most enjoyable visit we could have made. We were alone in the presence of some of the masters of the world. They spoke to us through the conception of their brains and the skill of their hands. It is impossible even to glance at the nearly two thousand paintings opened to you. Holbein and Dürer, Van Dyck and Rubens, Perugino and Correggio, Titian and Raphael, Tintoretto and Paul Veronese, had each worked for us, and we were alone in the presence of their best work. No footfall disturbed us; no whisperings of visitors; no dull explanations of guides, who have learned their lessons like parrots.

But at last we came to an artist; a genuine living artist, who had permission to perfect his work in the gallery. He was an old man, sitting before an easel on which was a half-finished painting of Abraham and Hagar. He was copying the painting by del Sarto.

The old artist's face was a study. I stopped to read his expression. He had evidently been dissatisfied with his work, and looked with delight and perplexity at the masterpiece. How could he ever get such coloring as distinguished the work of this renowned one of the Florentine school? He did not turn his head or avert his eyes one moment from his study. I walked out softly, not wishing to disturb him. It would be interesting to give the biography of an artist whose work, now nearly four hundred years old, has such power over the soul that the hours go by unnoticed by a devotee who can spend days in solitude, seeking to copy a single painting. He was a child of Florence, was married to a woman utterly unworthy of him, but for whom he always manifested the fondest attachment. His friends were astonished that her features were always prominent in the portraits of some of his most exalted characters. Did the artist's clear eye see beauty where others saw nothing but deformity? Is the critic correct who said: " He would have been a better artist if he had been more suitably married?"

The " Bavaria," a colossal monument, a short distance from the city, is esteemed by many an object of great interest. It is sixty-nine feet high, and there is a spiral stairway inside, which permits easy ascent, and through openings in the head, you can get a fine view. This is what we are taught in guide-books. I could not see the propriety of crawling up a stairway, through the chest and neck of the statue, in order to look out through little peep-holes, when you could stand outside, and see far more distinctly. But then there is a fee, a very small one, that is exacted of you for the privilege of going in to look out, and the easily gulled tourist thinks, of course, that a fee would not be charged, unless there was something to gain by its payment.

As we go south, the railway accommodations become better, or else we become accustomed to European fogyism. A hundred amusing things occur, and sometimes the joke comes too near home to be altogether pleasant. One's enjoyment of a joke depends very much on the person who is the chief sufferer from it. One day I went out hastily to have our luggage examined at the custom-house. I left my hat in the rack, wearing my traveling cap. After the fifteen minutes' worry of persuading the stupid officials that I had no dynamite with me, I was ushered into another compartment, and in fact into another train. I knew we were to change cars here, but had forgotten about my hat. On entering, I happened to put my hand to my head. The people in the compartment could not understand English, but they readily took in the situation; for one's annoyance at finding that he must travel without a hat, needs no interpreter to make plain. Of course, I blamed the doctor for not attending to my hat. He seemed glad that he had not allowed me to leave my coat and shoes. An Italian lady who sat opposite me, said something to her companion, and they both laughed, and then looked on me with a sort of pitying smile. I did not need an interpreter. I can endure ridicule, because of my mishaps, but smiling sympathy is too much for me. I was a foreigner, and even in America, enjoy jokes on someone else much better than on myself. The lady was elegantly dressed, and evidently belonged to the better class. If she had laughed outright and coarsely, I would have said that she was vulgar, and paid no more attention to it; but every time I put up my hand to my head, the lady looked out of the window, to hide her ridicule. That annoyed me still more. She was refined.

I recalled a little incident in Chicago, where a lady whose children did not care to be left in charge of the servant, got into a worse predicament. She had sent one of her servants out of the room with her children while she put on her hat and cloak, intending to avoid a scene with her little boys. She had just fastened on a face veil, when she heard the children coming back. She hastily left the house without ever thinking of her hat, and wearing the little veil, that stood up about her head like a crown.

Imagine, if you can, a lady elegantly attired, with a face veil, the rough upper edge of which is not covered by a hat. She walked to the street car, and entered it, for her trip down town, a distance of some three miles. People in the car seemed to be in an unusually good humor that morning. Everyone that came in, no matter how demure he was on entering, looked at her and was pleased. It was delightful to have this happy power of making others happy. At last a bright little woman looked at her, moved up beside her, and said, "Madam, pardon me. But really, you have forgotten to put on your hat!" The lady raised her hand, and then all the people in the car laughed aloud. What did she do? Get flurried and start back home? Not at all. She kept her seat, and when she got down town, walked into a store and borrowed a hat, and finished her shopping. I thought of her, and bided my time. Revenge came quickly, and terribly. There sat next to my tormentor, an old German lady, who carried a sort of catch-all, the mouth of which was opened, because the bag was too short to take in the whole length of a beer bottle which she carried. The motion of the car stirred up the nasty fluid, and as the cork went whizzing across the compartment, the beer sputtered out of the bottle on the frock, which was a delicate dove-color, or moonlight on the lake, or ashes of roses—I am unable to tell just what. I did not laugh. I said nothing. I was too deeply filled with regret to laugh—regret that the doctor had not been sitting beside her to have shared her fate. He enjoyed all, but suffered nothing. At the next stop, I sprang out of the train, and gave a few pfennigs to a man who pointed out another man, who also took a few more pfennigs, who showed me another man, carrying my hat, who handed it to me with a smile, caused by the pfennigs which I gave him. I returned in triumph, wearing my hat, while the lady sat with her stained dress, looking entirely subdued, and the doctor refused to recognize my good fortune, but seemed absorbed in the contents of a German paper, which he had bought in my absence. Some people in this life seem to be favored by escaping the misfortunes of their neighbors, even when they deserve punishment.

CHAPTER VII

E are nearing Venice. Who has not read of it? Who has not heard of the canals and gondolas and Rialto and Bridge of Sighs and palaces? I had dreamed of Venice, but scarcely dared entertain a hope of ever seeing it. Will I be disappointed? As we approach the city we look from both sides of the car, and the waters of the Adriatic are about us. For miles we are running over the sea. I remember the description. "Venice is built on seventy-two little islands in the great lagoon that is thirty miles long and five miles broad." It is raining, and the smooth waters about us are all dimpled, as it were, with smiles to greet us. We have reached the station. The porter of the Grand Hotel takes our luggage. I wished that we were some place else, where we could get a carriage, for there are no hacks here, and no horses, and to ride in a gondola in such a storm would not be pleasant. A gondola is called, and in a minute we are in a little compartment, the windows of which we draw to, and care not a farthing now where we are taken, and just as little whether it rains or shines. The gondolier pushes away from the steps, and glides past a score of other gondolas. He has received his directions from the hotel porter. We see but little of the city from our narrow coop. The rain increases, and the great drops of hail rattle against the windows. We are indifferent to hail and rain alike.

The poles in front of hotels and houses perplex us. We knew, of course, that there had to be something there with which to fasten the gondolas, but why should there be half a dozen in front of one house? Some, standing up out of the water, look for all the world like barber poles. They are striped, red and white. I told my friend that these striped poles showed a barber shop near by. He wanted to know why they needed eight poles for a single shop. Some people are unreasonable. They always make objections when you talk knowingly. The eight poles are simply a big sign. Some advertisers use an inch, others a column, and still others an entire page. This fellow is a big advertiser. He makes a display. At last we found out that these extra poles were used to keep the gondolas from floating out, crosswise, in the canal. The doctor was triumphant, and intimated that some people get age without getting wisdom. He could not mean me, for I was learning rapidly. So I said it was too true, and they were to be pitied, but I would continue teaching him, so that he need not fear it—for himself—and if there was anything else he did not understand, I would not think it any trouble to explain it to him. He looked at me in astonishment, but made no reply. After dinner, I walked out on the piazza, which is skirted by the waters of the Grand Canal. A gentleman, who spoke fairly good English, came to me, hurriedly, and said:

"Ah, Signor, do you know him? I thought you were a stranger; but I see you looking at him."

"I am looking at that splendid dog, standing on the front of the gondola."

"But, Signor," he continued, "the man in the gondola is Don Carlos, of Spain."

I did not want to show too much surprise, and so said:

"What a beautiful dog! He stands there as gracefully as if he were manning the gondola, and he has Don Carlos in the boat with him! The aspirant to the throne ought to be proud of such a dog!"

But, seriously, I doubted whether the dog, if he could reason, would be proud of his master.

You can go anywhere in Venice by little narrow alleys, called streets. On these the shops are situated, and from them bridges reach across the canals. These streets are tortuous and very narrow. You never see a horse or carriage in the city. If you will picture to yourself a city where the main streets are water and the alleys are dry land, and bridges across the main streets, so as to connect the alleys, you have a fair idea of the streets and canals of Venice. The great thoroughfare is the Grand Canal. It is in the shape of a letter *S*, and divides the city into nearly equal parts. There are one hundred and forty-seven small canals, spanned by about four hundred bridges. Our first trip was by the rear of the hotel, in a way so narrow that, in places, you could easily touch both walls at the same time, by extending your arms. The street itself which was filled with shops of different kinds, was not more than twelve feet wide.

We were anxious to hear from home, and so sought out the telegraph office. A friend had prepared a full code for us, so that by the use of a single word, we could ask or receive the answer to a question. You find, when cabling, that every word you use, including your name and address, and the name and address of the party to whom you telegraph, is charged for; hence the use of a code, where one word may mean very much. The message we sent was simply:

Patten, Chicago:
VILLAGE.

We did not sign our names to it, and gave no address in the city. The only thing the company does for nothing is, give the name of the city from which you send the message, and this they have to do for their own protection. The interpretation of our message was:

J. A. Patten, Chicago, Illinois, U. S. A.

Please cable us here at once, whether our families are well.

C. G. DAVIS.

W. T. MELOY.

It was six o'clock in the evening, and we knew that it was early in the afternoon at home, and that the message would be received before our Chicago friend left his office. Next morning we had the reply:

Meloy, Venice:

VILLA.

Which meant, with our full address, and the name of our friend.

Both your families are well.

Cyrus Field is dead, but I thanked God, for the first time in my life, that he once lived. How ungrateful we are! How near he brings us to our homes and loved ones! Italy is almost in speaking distance of Chicago.

The next place to visit is St. Mark's Square, which is simply a large open court, in front of St. Mark's Church. This church is joined to the Palace of the Doges. On the other sides, there are stores and shops and restaurants. All sorts of goods are sold here, the shop-keepers being skilled in remembering the customers who have visited them in former times, and gratifying their vanity by either naming them or giving some circumstances connected with a former visit. Such a recognition generally insures a purchase. In the shops we find Venetian glass, lace, carved wood, pictures, statuary, and jewelry. These are displayed in an artistic manner, and, while beautiful in themselves, appear doubly so as seen in Venetian settings. In the day-time thousands of pigeons gather in the square to be fed. Strangers buy little packages of corn, and the birds flock to the opened hand, tumbling over each other, on the palm and wrist of the one who feeds them, in their eagerness. Kindness, like love, casts out fear from the hearts, both of pigeons and men.

The Cathedral of St. Mark dates back to the tenth century, and is unlike any other cathedral in Europe. This may, in part, be accounted for by the fact that every vessel that came from the East, to Venice, was required to bring something for the church. There must have been a rivalry to secure the finest pillars and the richest pieces of marble. There are, in the front of the structure, five hundred columns, differing in size and shape and color. Within, are the pillars of solid alabaster, that appear to be over twelve inches in diameter, through which the light of a little taper may be seen more clearly than had the pillars been of glass. The first objects to which attention is invited, are the bronze horses, brought from Constantinople in the times of the crusades. They are not so wonderfully impressive that attention would be given them, were it not for their historic associations. Napoleon carried them away to Paris, but they were restored to Venice again in 1815, and it is probable that they will always remain here.

The ducal palace, ordinarily called the Doge's Palace, is an object of great interest. The name, *doge*, seems to be from the Latin *dux*—a leader. The name of the Rialto, so often used in all the world, was originally the name of one of the islands on which the city is built—the Island of Rivo Alto, the deep stream. There is a silly story, generally believed, that the Pope was so grateful to the Doge Ziani for withdrawing from a league against Barbarossa, that he gave him a ring, and joined the sea as a dutiful bride to Venice. The sea was ever afterward to be subject to the authority of her husband. But, somehow, things got reversed in the popular mind, and Venice has been called, not the husband, but the bride of the sea. It may be that the question of the rights of the bride became involved, and peace was gained, as in some other things, by a simple change of authority.

The Hall of the Great Council is one of the finest in Europe. It is one hundred and seventy-five feet long, eighty-five feet wide, and fifty-one feet high.

On the entrance wall is a picture of Paradise, by Tintoretto, which is the largest oil-painting in the world. It is eighty-four feet long, and thirty-four feet wide. Such a work would have been enough for an ordinary life-time, yet it is only one of hundreds that bear the artist's name. In this hall are the portraits of seventy-six doges. There is one space left vacant. It was made for the portrait of Marino Falieri, the fifty-sixth Doge. The space is painted black, and on it are the words, easily translated, because of their resemblance to the English, *Spazio di Marino Falieri, decapito.* There is something about this story, more than five centuries old, that awakens, even now, in our minds, strange feelings of interest. The Doge had been, before his appointment to office, singularly successful in maintaining the honor of Venice, both as statesman and warrior. When eighty years old, he was called on to accept the governorship of Venice. Adverse fortune overtook the fleets of the brave people. But, with consummate skill, he made honorable treaties, and his reign gave promise of a close in peace. The Doge gave a great feast in the palace, which was the more enjoyed because of the successful terms of a truce established with Genoa. A young man, Michael Steno, insulted, at this revel, one of the maids of honor, which so offended the Doge that he ordered the youth to quit the palace. The young and unprincipled

Steno sought revenge by writing a mean charge on the Doge's chair, against the wife of the Doge himself. Steno was tried, and the severity that prevailed then seemed, for some reason, to have been relaxed, and he received a few weeks of imprisonment and but one year's exile. This so outraged the haughty old Doge that he madly determined to wreak summary vengeance on all the nobility of Venice. He knew that in their slaughter he would have the sympathy of the people, for the nobility were hated as tyrants. But, before the time fixed for executing his purpose, the plot was discovered. He was arrested, and made full confession. The council ordered him to be beheaded. Under the great stairs of the palace, which we have looked on, the sentence was executed, and now the space, intended for his portrait, is blank.

We must respect the Doge's great age and great services to the state. We must honor him for rebuking the insult offered to a maid of honor. We praise his righteous indignation at the insult offered to his wife. We may even regard the sentence passed on the Venetian nobleman as wholly inadequate. But the great crime he contemplated was altogether unjustifiable. His sentence may have been just, but we can not look on the vacant space without feeling that justice is terrible, and experiencing a regret that the space should remain there to tell coming centuries a story that otherwise might have been forgotten. The feeling is intensified when, some hours later, we stand in the dark, cold cell where the old man was confined.

Lord Byron has written an historical tragedy, based on this sad history. He represents the Doge as an educated, patriotic ruler; yet rash and violent. He gathers the conspirators about him and denounces the gross insult offered to him. He denounces the forty for the mere semblance of punishment inflicted on one who had dared to insult the wife of the ruler. But at last, being condemned, he refuses to plead for mercy, and forgives his enemies, but defies the court that had condemned him. Then he begins an oration, that becomes more bitter as he proceeds to record the city's ingratitude, and turns, with a malediction on his lips, to the executioner, whom he thus addresses:

> " Slave to thine office !
> Strike as I struck the foe ! Strike as I would
> Have struck those tyrants ! Strike deep as my curse !
> Strike—and but once ! "

We are getting away from those days of injustice and cruelty. Humanity turns not to the East for its wisdom and guidance, but he who reads the history of the race, and marks the signs of the times, must recognize that a fuller, clearer, sweeter light has dawned upon the world. The black veil, painted over the vacant place, may never be removed, and the world may still hear the sad story of an old man's wrath and cruel death, but the head that fell w.s crowned only with that poor symbol of authority which a people can give and which they may take away again. The Jews cried out, centuries before this, "We have no king but Cæsar!" The nations of the earth will yet become republics, and, in the high freedom which enlightened and redeemed natures enjoy, will send back to the East a mighty shout, which all people shall hear, "We have no king but Jesus!" And, in that reign, he who has served most will be most honored, and part of the honor will be greater ability for doing more, and fuller opportunity for service. I turn away from the pictures of the doges, and from the palaces, too, rejoicing that America has no palaces, no titled nobility, no royal pensioners, no untaxed lands, no kings, and no slaves!

We returned to the hotel, where we found many Americans at table. They greeted us as though we had always been friends. They all seemed happy, but one. She was a woman who had evidently been disappointed in life, and, as she was now past fifty, saw no opportunity to recover lost ground, so she gave herself up to criticism and wine. She saw no beauty in Venice; flowers had no fragrance; the skies were not bright, even in Italy, and there was nothing fair in all the world, and nothing good in any man, or in anything. I smiled, in approbation of her decision, when she said, that after all she had concluded to remain twelve months longer in Venice, for I was afraid she might visit Chicago.

The sun was setting in a cloudless sky when we ordered a gondola to the steps. We are to see Venice by night, and that night a moonlight. The gondolier lighted his lamp and rowed his boat out on the Grand Canal. There seemed to be no twilight, for the moon began to silver over the waters as soon as we had seen the sun disappear. Here and there her beams were hidden by some palace, and when we were in the shadows the darkness was intense. The lights of a hundred lamps, shining from as many gondolas, seemed unreal, in their weird beauty. We heard the strange calls of the gondolier, as he indicated his course or directed his fellows on their way. His shadow, with the long oar in his hand, was projected at great length on the waters. He takes a short, noiseless dip of the oar, and balancing himself and guiding his boat at the same time, seems to know where to hesitate and where to speed you on. The merry voices of pleasure-seekers, as they flit by, tell you of different nationalities seeking to gain favor from the same shy goddess—Pleasure. It is easy to distinguish the German, French, and Italian. Now we meet a gondola containing six persons, who have no secrets

to keep, and again only two, who whisper words of
love, from trembling lips, that can only be understood as the heart becomes interpreter. They have
instructed their gondolier to go very softly through
the shadows, or does the wise Venetian know to
linger there without directions? We hear the sweet
voices of the natives, who have trained themselves
to catch liras from strangers, as they sing their lyrics.
We glide by old palaces of wealth and refinement,
and by simpler homes, where, on the balconies over
the canal, friends are talking with each other. We
pass by the same houses of which Shakespeare wrote.

The gondolier, bending forward, attempts to tell us
in English, the names of palaces and the bridges that
span the smaller canals. Under the Rialto, and then
by tortuous ways, by many a turn in narrower waters,
calls out, at length, "*Ponte de' Sospiri.*" It would
have been irreverent to have said "the Bridge of
Sighs." But we would have known it had he not
given it a name. Here is the structure over which,
from the palace to the prison, so many sad hearts have
gone. The bridge is much higher than the others,
and never was used for a general thoroughfare, for the
sufficient reason that to enter it one must have first
been in the prison or the palace. There is a popular
error that this bridge led to the old dungeons. The

old dungeons are under the palace, and before the
year 1620 prisoners were confined in them.

It was nine o'clock in the evening, and we ordered
our gondolier, with a single word, to take us to St.
Marks. All Venice seemed to be there; America,
England, France, and Germany were there. A band
was discoursing sweet music in the center of the
square. A thousand men and women were prom-
enading, chatting eagerly, or listening to the music.
The cares of the home and the shop were left behind
by these. The irritations of the day were forgotten,
and the quarrels of friends and lovers were easily adjusted in the midst of this gaiety. Two thousand were
filling the shops or sitting at tables, eating and drinking. A beer, that must have been light, from the vast
mugs in which it was served, was the favorite beverage.
Many, however, contented themselves with mineral
waters and lemonades. There was no loud talking,
and no boisterous behavior. Beautiful ladies, who
knew how to add to their charms by the skillful
adjustment of the laces thrown over their heads,
enjoyed the rest, and as they emptied their goblets,
had an opportunity of studying the characters and
habits of wanderers from over the world. The story
of the beauty of refined Italian ladies is not overdrawn; but there is a lack of that sprightliness and

intelligence that distinguish women in the British Isles and in America.

After a few hours we returned to our hotel, and sought sleep. The little child, unused to scenes of gaiety, sometimes banishes the angel that soothes it to rest. It was so with me. I lived the evening over again many times before I closed my eyes, and then would waken from the dream of the gently dipping oar and flickering light that turned the waters into brightness and beauty, and of sweet strains of music and shadowy forms of graceful men, bending to the oar. I heard again the gondolier's call, as in the darkness he turned about the corners of a palace. I slept, dreamed, and awoke again. Then I rubbed my eyes, and muttered, "Beautiful Venice! Seen by night, with her heart bent on pleasure! Can the dream be repeated by day, or will the light cause the picture to fade away? There are nobler objects in life than mere pleasure. I have drawn the picture by artificial light, and if the sun destroy it, I shall experience a disappointment."

I found in a paper, published in the West, an account of our night in Venice, from the pen of my companion, Doctor Davis. The reader, I know, will thank me for giving his impressions, in his own well-dressed sentences.

ONE NIGHT IN VENICE.

Ah, classic Venice! We dreamed of it in our boy-
hood days. We saw it in our imagination, and linked
it with the romances of our earlier years. We are
met at the station by the porter of our hotel. He
conducts us through the throng of people. What a
babel of tongues! Italian, French, German, and
English voices are heard mingling with the stranger
tones coming from the distant Orient. We go through
a labyrinth of passages to a landing, with steps of
stone leading down to the water's edge. On looking
up, we see a broad street, but it is water, and the houses
rise high on either side, showing marks made from the
rising and falling of the tide. Just at the water's
edge are a number of strange-looking boats, about
thirty feet long, tapering at each end and rising in
front to an ornamented crest, not unlike the curve of
a swan's neck. Most of them have a little canopy in
the center, large enough to protect two people. On
the rear of each stands a man shouting for customers.
Ah, we understand now; these are gondoliers with
their gondolas, waiting to take us to our respective
hotels. They are the cabmen of Venice. It is raining
and hailing. We draw down the glass sides of our
canopy, and are safe from the storm. Soon we are
gliding down the Grand Canal. The gondolier has but
one oar, and yet he steers the gondola with wonderful

7

precision.   We glide in and out between many
others on the canal, but there is no collision.   We
pass into a narrower channel, and under many bridges;
these are the causeways that connect the narrow foot-
streets in the rear of the canals.   The clouds disappear, the sun shines, and now we are nearing a series
of marble steps.   The water splashes upon them, the
gondola stops, and a courteous porter welcomes us to
the Grand Hotel.   We order dinner, repair to our
rooms, improve our toilets, and entering the drawing-
room find a number of pleasant Americans.   We
converse, and look out over the Adriatic Sea.

But the shades of evening are coming on, the lights
are appearing, and now is the hour when Venice,
" Queen of the Sea," robes herself like a joyous bride.
The sky is blue, the stars shine like jewels in the
vault of heaven, and the moon, nearing the full, casts
shadows of towering castles and spires, lighting up the
ivied walls, and reflecting back, in a thousand waves
of quivering light, the ripples of the Adriatic Sea.
We again enter our gondola, and say to our gondolier,
"the Grand Canal."   We are soon gliding over the
sparkling waters, from which a thousand lights and
fantastic shapes are reflected.   At each dip of the
oar, the water falls like a myriad of pearls, dimpling
on the surface, and the slight ripple is the only sound
that breaks the quiet calm.   But we are not alone.

Soon, from every direction, come gondolas in swarms. Venice, now, is on pleasure bent. She has awakened from her sleep. Some of the mysterious barks contain one, two, three, or even six people. Some of the occupants are riding in meditative thought, some are full of the joy of life, and send their songs of plaintive melody out over the waters, and still others whisper their words so low and soft that we can only imagine a recital of the old, old story. On and on we go, passing at every turn, monuments of painting, romance, and art, the castles of the old nobility, gliding down narrow canals, then into wider ones, under bridges, under the famed Rialto, and, at the last, under the historic Bridge of Sighs, across which, in past centuries, hundreds, perhaps thousands, of human beings have walked to the dungeons beneath the Palace of the Doges. As we glide under this arch, and between the palace and the old prison, the stillness is oppressive, and the very air seems laden with mysterious whisperings of those who, in these subterraneous cells, suffered agony and death. But ah, we are in the moonlight again, the air is full of soft strains of music, light, and life. Could it be possible for so much agony, pain, and death to have entered here?

We land, and approach the plaza of St. Mark's Church, Thousands are now coming here, to finish the night's revel. A band discourses music. We are again in the babel of tongues. We hear, the same instant, German, French, English, and Italian spoken. Some promenade, while others sit and listen to the ebb and flow of melody, or converse in quiet tones. There is no noise, no boisterousness; each individual seems tuned in harmony with the surroundings. It is nearing midnight; the crowd is gently dispersing; we seek our hotel. The music is dying out, but still, at intervals, from the Grand Canal, the palaces, and even far out on the Adriatic, some plaintive strain comes to mingle with our dreams. Venice, like a beautiful, happy child, is sleeping, pillowed on the sea.

August 5, 1892.

———

And now, what more shall I say of Venice? It would be pleasing to leave the reader with the delightful impression made on his mind by what has been given by my friend. Truthful words will surely offend. The lamps have gone out on the canals. Gondolas have lost a part of their charm. A smoking little steamer disturbs the waters of the Grand Canal. The bridges are old and ugly. The walls of the palaces are scaly, and remind me of potatoes with the skin all flecking off. The little narrow streets never see the sun, and are full of beggars. The city is old, grotesque, and without ambition. I experienced the little boy's disappointment, when, the morning after the circus, he goes to the grounds. The ring is there, but the tinseled riders are nowhere to be found. He sees heaps of old straw, where the night before a princess was crowned. Venice by night is the rocket that sweeps gracefully through the heavens and bursts in a blaze of glory, and astonishes again and again, by fresh exhibitions of brilliancy. Venice by day is the stick that falls with a dull thud to the ground when the rocket has exploded. It is the ashes left when the candle has burned low in the socket. It is the toy balloon that delighted the child yesterday, but is found in the morning wilted up in some corner of the room. It is a golden chariot by night, but in the morning it is without comeliness.

Yet I am glad that I saw Venice by night—by moonlight, for though, like the photographic proof, the sun may spoil it, yet I recall, with pleasure, the fair picture before the sun had touched it. Buy only colored pictures of Venice—moonlight scenes, if you can get them. The sun reveals the mold and scaling walls and poverty of a city that has no counterpart on earth. Yet, with it all, and after the lapse of a few months, the fair night scene grows brighter, and the reality of the day becomes less distinct. It is, however, in accordance with a higher law, that melodies are eternal, while discords are destroyed. One in love with

Venice will say of her, as the artist said of his wife, "Poverty can not hide her graces, for even in rags she would be nobler than a queen."

The next morning we visited the dungeons under the palace. In the upper dungeons criminal prisoners were kept. The walls were lined with wood, and the prisoner had a wooden slab on which to lie. He was generally allowed fifteen days after he was sentenced in which to prepare for death. The political prisoner was confined in a dungeon beneath the former. He was shut in by an iron door, and there was no wood whatever in his cell. His bed was a stone slab elevated a little above the floor. A few dim rays of light entered the cell, and the air was enough to make his imprisonment shorter than the time allotted him. He had but three days given him in which to prepare for judgment. In the gloomy hallway outside these cells, is a narrow stone on which thousands were beheaded. An opening in the floor near this stone allowed the blood of the slain to escape to the waters of the canal under the Bridge of Sighs. I began to deplore the cruelty of the doges, and did not see how such monsters could live in Venice. The guide responded, using three languages, and his words, as I interpreted them, were:

"Ah, Signor, that was six hundred years ago. Italy

does not hang men up by the thumbs now, as was done in America last month."

I found it convenient to resort to the usual trick of a servant we once had, who never understood English when told to do anything that she did not want to do. I failed to fully comprehend him. Yet, had I known all the circumstances, it would not have been hard to give an excuse for seeming cruelty. Severity is sometimes mercy. It is difficult for us to judge of what is done four thousand miles away, or of what was done five hundred years ago. Were we nearer, either in time or distance, we might excuse, or even justify, what we are so ready to condemn. But how little the world is! History gives us an ever present judgment-seat, from which we determine the quality of actions done in the remote past, and the telegraph enables the most distant nations to sit in judgment on the deeds of our yesterday.

CHAPTER VIII

O N the way to Milan, I jotted down the words:
"Beautiful lakes, old forts, poor fields."
The fact has been forcing itself on me
ever since we crossed the North Sea, that
Europe is impoverished by her standing armies.
Almost every ridge has been fortified at a vast
expenditure of labor and money. These fortifications,
so useful a few years ago in military struggles, are
to-day of little more value than the castles of feudal
lords. Science has rendered these forts of no use
whatever, unless it be to reveal what sacrifices men
made to overcome their fellows, or to retain their soil.
It seems almost a paradox, but it is true, that the more
destructive the enginery of war may be, the more
surely will it tend to peace. When the missile means
death, men will hesitate long before they resort to
its use.

It is not alone the vast sum that is paid to equip and
feed and pay an army, that drains away a nation's life.
These things are not little in the scale. The loss to a
country is incalculable when you draw away from its

producing force such armies as are maintained in Germany and France, and even in England. It retards the spread of general intelligence among the people, by lessening the number of the hands left to do the work of life. The children are neglected when the mother labors in the field. It is also to be noted that the army demands the strong and young and well-favored from among the people, and the drudgery of the camp gives but little time for study, and but little disposition for reflection. Work itself does not ennoble. It is enduring work that gives character to our toil. When the nations learn war no more, there will be possibilities for advancement that do not exist to-day. Time wasted, energies misdirected, treasures unprofitably employed, are the sure precursors of poverty and discontentment.

We come nearer the Alps, and as the evening approaches the mountains gaze on us with frowning brows. There were two things in Milan that caused us to visit it. The first, of course, was the cathedral, and the second a painting on the walls of a dingy little chapel. The cathedral, which has been the wonder of the world, we first saw by electric light. Having read so many descriptions of it, I felt a peculiar thrill of satisfaction, when, from my room, I looked out on the brilliantly lighted streets, and across the square, in plain view of my window, was the cathedral of Milan.

I had read in books that it has ninety-eight turrets, two thousand statues, and that the roof is supported by fifty-two columns, from eight to twelve feet in thickness, and that it has been in process of erection for more than five hundred years. It was a favorable time to see the great building, and in the bright lights its many minarets shone and glistened as if the pure white marble had been finely polished. But the first feeling I had was one of disappointment. Something impressed me unfavorably about it. You have a friend who never can be comfortable when in your presence, if there is anything wrong with your attire. He is restless if he sees a dent in your hat. He can hardly contain himself if your vest collar shows the sixteenth part of an inch above your coat. He gets fidgety if your neck-tie threatens to become unfastened. He wants to straighten you out just now and here, before he can enjoy life. Some such feeling took possession of me as I leaned on the window-sill and looked at the cathedral. But as it took five hundred years to build it, I had serious doubts whether, in the years allotted to me, I could have its proportions corrected. The building does not appear high enough for its width, and notwithstanding the fact that the top of the statue of the Madonna is three hundred and fifty-five feet above the pavement, the building looks too low. This may be caused by the unusual width of the cathedral (two hundred and eighty-seven feet), and also because the pinnacles in front hide the steeple in the center. As we walked about it by moonlight, and took in its vastness, this feeling was to some extent modified, but not entirely removed, and subsequent reflections deepen the impression first made. The floor is in mosaic of red, white, and blue marble. The greater part of the interior is taken up with monuments of prelates and relics of saints, which are interesting only as they tell us of the idolatry and superstition of Rome.

I witnessed a number of confessions, where kneeling women were pouring out their sorrow in the ears of priests, no doubt giving confidences that should have been given rather to their own husbands or fathers, or to God. I stood for a few minutes and witnessed the so-called religious service, where, amid smoking incense, these zealots were presumably worshiping God and adoring the Virgin.

I paid twenty-five centimes (five cents), and began the ascent of the tower. It is five hundred steps up, and they are not easily taken. Guides offered their services, but I did not see of what possible use they could be to me, yet, in places where I came out on the roof, and was confused by the number of minarets about and above me, it would have been a little more comfortable to have had someone tell me where to go next. I was walking slowly along the marble roof, when I met some Americans, and innocently asked them if I were near the top. The reply was that I had a full half-day's work before me. I said I thought that whatever work I had on hand just now was above me, while theirs seemed to be in the opposite direction. I went up above the dome, and above a forest of white minarets, that stood up like ice-covered pines on the mountain side. I laughed at myself for taking hold of the marble projections to see if they were secure, and yet I found myself doing this again and again, regardless of the ridicule I subjected myself to from myself, for I was alone.

At last the highest point was gained, and in wondering amazement I looked down on the spires below me. I was on a mountain top, and from this exalted position, I saw all about the mountain sides the snow-white minarets. They seemed to be numberless, and white as the wings of a dove, bathed in the full light of a noonday sun. The city of nearly three hundred and fifty thousand inhabitants appeared to be very little.

I am told, that as men rise the things from which they have risen seem small. It is not right, for that by which any one has risen should always be respected. The cathedral became a motherly hen, and the houses of Milan, like dutiful chickens, were gathered near, as if to be taken under her protecting wings.

Milan is one of the most modern wide-awake cities in Europe. The *Galleria Vittorio Emanuele*, near the cathedral, is a most inviting place. To us the name gave no idea of the place, and a description will necessarily be imperfect. It is a vast arcade, formed where two streets cross each other. For a distance of nearly one thousand feet these streets are covered over with high glass arches. Where the streets cross, there is a splendid dome, one hundred and eighty feet in height. The whole is in the form of a Latin cross. Along these covered ways are elegant shops and restaurants, and here and there are graceful statues by the sidewalks. Here, every evening in summer, the Milanese resort. It is the Square of St. Mark's repeated again. Milan is copying Venice. The same good order prevails here that does at Venice. It must also pay the city in a business way, for the shops in the arcade bring fabulous rents, and the city is careful to secure its full share of the revenue.

But Milan contains one treasure that no visitor should fail to see. Taking a street-car, we ask for the church of the Grazie (Graces), and hasten to the little chapel that contains the treasure. It is here that the great work of Leonardo da Vinci was executed. Here the ruins of that masterpiece are still to be seen. The fame of "The Last Supper" is world wide, and will be cherished when the work itself has perished, and naught but poor copies of it remain. The little chapel is uninviting, and it seems strange that on the wall of this building such skill should have been displayed. The picture was executed about the close of the fifteenth century. It was not appreciated as of any value, and has experienced some strange fortunes. It was badly smoked by a kitchen stove, probably flooded, parts of it cut away by the monks, who opened a doorway through the wall on which it was painted, and, if possible, a worse fate befell it when some stupid artists attempted to restore it. The wall on which it is painted is scaling off, and taking flecks of the figures along with the scales.

I had regarded the enthusiasm excited by this picture as mere sentiment. Anyone will have the same feeling who judges it by the copies that are to be found in every city. I was disappointed when I looked on it from a distance. The mark paid for admission seemed to be wasted. But coming nearer I took a chair and sat down deliberately to study the world-renowned painting. The pose and expression of the different figures impressed me. I found myself saying, almost aloud:

"What beauty in the repose of that sweet face!"

"What wonderful mildness of expression!"

"How symmetrical the hand that lies opened with the palm turned upward!"

"See the cups partly filled with wine, and the scattered fragments of bread !"

I never saw a picture that appealed to me as this one did. How could the stupid monks fail to see its beauty? How could even the common soldiery of Napoleon fail to be touched with the pictured gentleness of that Blessed One who said, "Put up thy sword, for all that take the sword shall perish by the sword?"

Yet there are some things to criticise. Ruskin would have all pictures true. But here the figures are all conveniently arranged so that the artist could take them in; not one of them is reclining, as was the custom at Eastern meals. John is leaning away from Jesus, and not on his breast.

The painting is now nearly four hundred years old, and it looks as though in ten years more it might be entirely lost. Thus it is with all the works of man. They perish. The strong castle, built by rough hands, and the delicate touches of the brush must pass away, but the colorings of light and shade left on human hearts will endure. The painting can not outlast the canvas or the wall, and human skill finds its limit here. He who influences one life for good is the greatest artist, and produces the most enduring work. That influence may be exerted by tongue or pen or brush, or by the unspoken sympathy of a soul that

substitutes a look for a word. A half-dozen artists were
seated before this painting, making copies of it. We did
not stop to examine their work, though it was fresh and
easily seen. When da Vinci's work was before us,
why should we linger a minute at the side of a mere
copyist? After seeing his work, I did not wonder that
in the beautiful Plaza della Scala, at the end of the
arched street, of which I have written, there should
be a fine monument to da Vinci, with busts of his
most eminent pupils about it. The fairest monument,
however, he erected for himself in "The Last Supper,"
and universal regret must be felt that it was neglected
so long, and that it must perish so soon.

Good-by to Italy, with its bright skies, into whose
far-away depths I have looked for an hour. Why did
we not linger here another month? Ten years would
be all too few to satisfy the soul that delights in com-
munion with all that is fairest in art. The friend
lingers an hour beyond the allotted time, and finds it
much harder then to step beyond the threshold than
he would have done had he departed when the moment
arrived. The land that is richest in art is debased by
superstition. May she be freed from it and enlightened by the sweet simplicity of Gospel truth! We
hasten to the land of Tell.

Switzerland is the playground of Europe and the
resting place for America. When Germany and

England have a cholera fright, they hurry off to Switzerland. When the heat becomes oppressive, Parisians seek Alpine villages. It is a relief to get away from man's work to God's, away from paintings to snow-clad mountains and bold rivers and frightened cascades. Switzerland is only a little country, not being twice as large as New Jersey, and most of it is composed of mountains and lakes. But the world would be far less beautiful if Switzerland did not form a part of it. From Milan to Lucerne, by the St. Gotthard Road, is a distance of one hundred and seventy-six miles, and the time of travel is about ten hours. It seems as though this were slow traveling, but if you will take the ride you will be thoroughly convinced that the rate of speed is sufficiently high for the safety of the passengers and for their comfort as well.

The engineering skill displayed on the St. Gotthard Road is not excelled anywhere. The engine boldly enters a mountain, as one would suppose, to find its iron pathway directly through it, but this would be impossible, for the tunnel would need to be many miles long before the proper grade could be reached. In place, therefore, of going directly through the mountain, it winds up in a curved tunnel on the inside, making, in one instance, near *Dazio Grande*, two complete loops. Imagine a corkscrew road, with two turns inside the mountain, and you have the best illustration

8

that can be given in words. Going from Milan, the
road pierces the mountain and comes out again at a
higher level, after making the inside curves, and if
you are going in the opposite direction, the train
winds down in place of up the tunnel. Yet the road
is so well constructed that there is as little jarring as
there is on any of our roads built on the plain.

A finely educated gentleman from Greece sat in the
compartment with us. He spoke all languages probably better than English. I thought it was a splendid
chance to brighten up a little in German with him.
I even ventured to tell him a little pleasantry we have
in our home about my having five boys, while my wife
claims that she has six. I knew he understood me, for
he laughed heartily and wakened up the interest of a
Spaniard who was in the compartment. The gentleman told the story to him in Spanish, and it so amused
him that he reached over and took my hand and said
something that I did not understand, and which may
have meant:

"That is a very stupid thing to tell," but I interpreted it to mean:

"You are a good fellow and I am glad to ride in
the same compartment with you."

Then I looked over at the doctor, who was reading
a Swiss paper, and caught his eye. He was disgusted
with me. He even suggested, in a modest way, that

when I was conversing with an educated gentleman who spoke English as well as I did, he would be somewhat prouder of me if I would not persist in cramming my broken Dutch on him. I saw in a moment that the doctor was jealous of my accomplishments and felt it his duty to humble me. I did not humble, but kept on talking to the professor in German, using the masculine pronoun for the feminine, and both of them for the neuter, and making such blunders that I finally disgusted the doctor, and at the next stop he left the compartment. I am sure that I did the best I could, and the professor told me that if I would study I could become an expert in talking German. I suppose he meant that I would not be so modest that I would refuse to speak it.

Then I fell into a serious mood of reflection. How does it come that we always want to do something that we can not do? I think that the doctor wants to preach. I suggested to him, that as I knew so much about diagnosticating diseases, I would study medicine with him. He reminded me of several times that I had mistaken mumps for chicken-pox, and rheumatism for consumption. I could not remember the instances, but they were firmly fixed in his mind, so I marked this down to jealousy again. But why he should be jealous of my German, I could not imagine, so I sought him out in the other compartment, and asked him to explain himself. When he gave me a full interpretation of his feelings, I was so much humiliated, that I refused to leave the compartment again. Some of his friends had brought in a basket of fruit, and I had accepted an invitation to share it with him. The scholar must have missed me.

We were in the midst of the Alps, and the clouds began to gather about the mountain-tops. I had spoken of the forces of the air mustering there, and expected the doctor to compliment me on the elegance of the figure. He was in a poetical mood, and observed that the clouds were quite demonstrative. Someone asked how. He replied that they were kissing the mountain's brow.

I supposed that they only kissed the brow because the mountain was older than the clouds, and they wanted to be reverent, like the young wife of an old husband, who tries to kiss away the wrinkles. It began to rain, and I proposed a conundrum.

" Why are the clouds like Jacob ? "

No one seemed to know much about Jacob, except that he had stolen Esau's blessing, so I had to explain that he wept after the osculatory process with Rachel.

Below us was the sweet Valley of the Ticino, but a few rods wide. The Swiss have cultivated every foot of land along the stream, and up as far on the mountain-side as possible. It looked like a well-kept garden. Cottages here and there could be seen, but it is evident that the owners of the little half-acre farms live in villages, and these subject to avalanches, which cause great loss of life and property. There are drawbacks to the fairest portions of earth. The delightful roads of Continental Europe and the splendid railways have been built by a people who have lived on the coarsest food and received beggarly wages. If Europe paid less to her armies, and less to sustain a pensioned nobility, that neither toils nor spins, she would not have to withhold wages, fair and adequate, from her toilers. I am glad that labor in America is not pauperized, and am quite willing to pay duties on all I wear, if need be, rather than see my countrymen toiling as the people do in the East. (This was written before the election of 1892.) I have seen women cutting grass with the scythe, and when it was loaded on the cart, hitched to it, along with a dog and a cow, to haul it to the stable. The men are in the army, and poverty is in rags, to support soldiers, and noblemen, and royalty. Poetry becomes dull prose, and titles lose their dignity, when seen in the light of unrewarded toil. The law given in Holy Writ ought to be maintained throughout the world: "If any toil not, neither shall he eat;" and "The laborer is worthy of his hire."

We left the train at Fluellen, on Lake Lucerne, and

embarked on a steamer for Lucerne. Here we met many tourists, whom we had seen at different places. These pleasant greetings began now to form an important part of the pleasures of our tour :

" We were together on the *Brittanic* ! "

" We met in Venice ! "

" I saw you in London ! "

I wondered if, when we get to heaven, we will recall those with whom we have passed a salutation on earth !

Will some kind stranger say,

" I always wanted to meet you, since something you said, or wrote, with tear-dimmed eyes, has shed a ray of light on my path, and helped me to get here ? "

The ride by steamer was a delight, after the nine hours on the train. We passed by Tell's Chapel and Schiller's Rock; looked up to the Rigi on the one hand, and to Pilatus on the other, and just at dark arrived at the beautiful little city of Lucerne, with its many hotels, clustering about the western end of the lake. We were very fortunate in finding every room of the down-town hotels occupied, and were compelled to go to the *Hotel de l'Europe*, some distance east. Here we secured rooms fronting the lake, and from our windows we looked across the quiet waters to the mountains, clothed in white. The rising moon gave an added charm to the far-off mountain, while its light fell, in a silvery baptism, on the waters of Lucerne.

The guests at the hotel had retired, the noise on the street had ceased; yet I sat, a lone watcher, by my window, and looked at the wondrous scene. In mute admiration, I worshiped Him "who giveth snow like wool," and causeth "the moon to shine by night." Words would have been a mockery at such an hour, as they could not have expressed the emotion of the soul.

The rest day came in Lucerne, and we sought out a school-hall, where Presbyterian services were held. It was in an out-of-the-way place, and almost everything about the service was out of the way. The singing was poor, and the sermon was in perfect harmony with the music. For some reason or other, the preacher felt that he would not be at home unless he wore a gown. A gown in Presbyterian circles is getting to be stylish, and possibly the taste in this direction is not to be condemned; although a manly dress is always more becoming to a man than a womanly one. But, in this case, the preacher's gown was one to attract attention. It was mussed up, and wrinkled, and looked as though it might have been as long in a little hand-bag as Jonah was in the fish. It is always painful to me to see a minister make himself ridiculous by appearing clerical, under any circumstance, and specially so when the attempt is as silly as the desire. I had been looking at the comely in nature, and was in no mood to tolerate the uncomely in art. The surroundings, and wrinkled gown, and poor music, would have made it impossible for a man to preach well. He did not attempt the impossible.

After sermon we sat down to lunch, when, to our surprise and pleasure, Mr. and Mrs. Case, whom we had met at The Hague, came in, and sat at our table. It was a most pleasant meeting for us. The doctor had occasion to render some professional services, which were highly appreciated, and he did not have to wait many days to get a return for the bread he was casting on the waters.

I proposed to the doctor that we take a bath in the lake, next morning, early. He agreed, and Mr. Case was to join us. The lake looked cold, and I had no idea that my proposal would be accepted, or I would not have made it. I wanted to appear courageous, and tell them how refreshing it would be. I studied several plans to disconcert the agreement, but all to no avail. I began to get interested in the doctor's health, and told him the early bath, in the cold water, might be injurious to him.

He looked incredulous.

I suggested that it might bring on neuralgia, or rheumatism, or sciatica, or jumping toothache. My medical talk spoiled it all. If he were about to yield before, he refused now and became firm. It would be invigorating and better than any tonic. He needed it, and he knew that it would aid my circulation, sending the blood spinning all through my body. It would be specially helpful to me in using the German language. I consented when he said this, knowing how eager he was for my welfare, but inwardly resolved that it would not be convenient for me to be awake next morning before eight o'clock. But even this last resort failed, for I overheard him giving directions to the porter, that we should be called at six.

When we reached the bath-house, Mr. Case had already taken his plunge and was about to retire. I hurried into the lake first. It is so hard, when water is cold, to get wet all at once, and I wanted to help the doctor get used to it gradually by throwing a few handfuls at him from long range. The plan worked to perfection, only for some reason he did not seem to appreciate my kindness as highly as he might have done. But having heard that we ought not to cease our good offices because of man's ingratitude, I did not desist until he was swimming gracefully far beyond his depth. The water was as clear as crystal. When about to come out, I was horrified to see my friend, with a look of pain on his face, swimming toward me with one hand. His left arm was dislocated, and only because he was at home in the water, was he able to reach me in safety. It was to me strange, that, able to use but one arm, and suffering as he did, he gained the shore at all. Mr. Case took charge of him while I dressed hastily and set off to find a physician. Remember, if you please, that we were in Lucerne, where not one person in a hundred knows a single word of English. A surgeon, however, was secured, and he, after examining the dislocation, sent for an assistant. It seemed an age to wait, but while we waited the doctor's face suddenly brightened up, and he declared that the ball had gone back into its socket again. It was true, and when the second surgeon arrived with a can of chloroform, there was nothing for him to do.

I may be uncharitable, but I thought I saw on the second surgeon's face a look of disappointment. When he was informed, however, that the patient was a physician, he rejoiced with us and was full of congratulations, I suppose, for he spoke in a foreign tongue. There was a learned discussion as to how the happy result had been secured without surgical aid. The theory that he had touched the bones of some old saint was not favorably received, for this would have implied that he had not been in good company when I was with him in the water.

Every visitor at Lucerne is expected to ascend the

Rigi. The journey is easily made by the cog-wheel road up the mountain side. Taking the boat to Vitznau, a little town on the lake, we began the ascent, which occupied one hour and twenty minutes. The word *Rigi* means strata, and in climbing the mountain, the appropriateness of the name becomes apparent. But the Rigi is only five thousand nine hundred and five feet high, and therefore does not come up to the shoulders of Pike's Peak. But the singularly isolated position of the mountain gives a view that is said to be three hundred miles in circumference. As I did not make the circuit, I will not be responsible for the accuracy of the figures.

If one anticipate ruggedness on the Rigi he will be disappointed, particularly by this route. The mountain sides are, in some places, precipitous, but, to the highest point, the grass is growing, and cattle and sheep are feeding. But the general impression is favorable, and as you look away in the distance to the white-robed Jungfrau, whose snowy vesture has never been touched by mortal hand, you do not wonder why every tourist ascends the Rigi. Hotels are on the summit, and many tourists remain over night, to see the sun rise on the far-off mountains. But it has a habit of raining there so often, and the sun rises as early as four o'clock, and considering these things, and being also reasonably well persuaded that the

sun would be prompt, without our efforts, we concluded to sleep in the valley.

Very near the city is the Lion of Lucerne. This is
a bas-relief, cut in the solid rock—not in a rock hewn
from the quarry, but in its natural bed, on the mountain side. It is twenty-eight feet long, and is in com-
memoration of the bravery of the Swiss guard who
fell defending the Tuilleries, on August 10, 1792. It
was celebration week when we were at Lucerne, and
the little city was full of enthusiasm. The poverty of
the display made was in strange contrast with the
sacrifice offered. But as that offering was in defense
of royalty, the Republic of France could not be
expected to unite with Switzerland in honoring the
two qualities which go to make up the great soldier—
bravery and fidelity even to death.

We did not omit a visit to the Glacier Garden,
hard by the Lion's Rock. Here you are pointed out
many glacial mills, as they are called. They look
like great pots made in the solid rocks, by the action
of the ice rivers in the long ago. Some of them are
about fifteen feet in depth, and the sides show that
they have been ground out by revolving stones. It
is probably true that there was a time when a great
part of the Northern Hemisphere was buried under
mighty masses of ice. But the teachings of science are
somewhat peculiar, as one of the most distinguished

geologists in America is instructing us that the earth is slowly growing colder, and that, after awhile, it will be uninhabitable. Under these conditions a long lease would be quite as good a title as a deed of general warranty. But I am perplexed in attempting to reconcile this teaching with the ice-field theory.

It was our purpose to get as near Mount Blanc as we could, and we therefore started in that direction, arriving at the village of Martigny late in the evening.

CHAPTER IX.

THE route to Inter Laken may be richly varied by railway and boat, and will, as a pleasing picture, linger in memory with ever increasing delight. There comes to me now, as if in a panorama, the last sight of Lucerne, as the boat carried us over the lake to Alpnachstadt. A lingering look at Pilatus and the Rigi, and this part of the picture is folded away. The scenery on the route to Brienz is not so wild as you will find on the Rocky Mountains, but it is wonderfully varied, and as one looks down at the Aare, he feels that the swiftly flowing river has been sent in haste on some errand, and is already belated, and eagerly seeks to out-do its past record.

Scores of handsome cascades are leaping down the mountain-sides, some of which start out bravely, but are turned to mist long before they fall on the rocks below, where they are again collected, and flow on to the river as though they had not been broken to pieces by the fall, and lost to sight in the descent. Some wind down the rocks like silver threads, while many

(126)

of larger volume go with the ardor of the race-horse, that spurns the earth, and scatters the white foam from his widely extended nostrils.

The scenery of the Brünig Pass has been so often described, that the traveler is prepared in some degree for the delights afforded him. At Brienz we take the steamer for Inter Laken, passing Giessbach, justly famed for the beautiful falls of a stream, whose source is in the Schwarzhorn Mountain. There are seven of these falls, the highest one being eleven hundred and forty-eight feet above the lake. The lowest one can be seen from the steamer. Inter Laken, as its name imports, is between two lakes, on a low land that has probably been formed by the soil washed down from the mountain-sides, thus dividing the great lake in two parts, one of which is called Brienz, and the other Thun.

We took an evening drive by a pleasant road, passing through a Swiss village, into whose cottages we were permitted to get an occasional glance. That look convinced us that the tidiness which has been so generally accorded to the Swiss may at least have some exceptions. A heavy rain came on, and while we drove along, we saw many carts loaded with hay. The women who had been pulling in the loads had stopped by the way-side, and sought shelter under the carts. I was glad to see that there was this much advantage afforded them over the horses and cattle, which would have been compelled to remain in the rain. There is something better in the lot of a woman in Switzerland than there is in the condition of an ox. The woman can disengage herself, and get under her load, while the ox must remain in the harness.

We had planned for a visit to the Rhone Glacier, but the tourist in Switzerland must be prepared for many disappointments, or else take many excursions which he can not enjoy, because of the rains. The visit to the glacier was abandoned, and possibly it would not have been my good fortune to write these lines, if we had done this, for many idiots are lost every year when attempting to cross the rivers of ice.

The ride by boat and cars to Martigny is not so full of interest as that which we have passed over, but it is necessary to be at Martigny, to secure passage over the Tête-Noire Pass, to Chamounix, the evening before you make the journey. Here we met Miss Halsted, and her party, who had been wrecked on the ill-fated *City of Chicago*. We were kindly permitted to join their party, and together we secured carriages for Chamounix.

The morning was delightful, and the scenery was largely a repetition of what we had enjoyed before. The distance is only twenty-three miles, but owing to the grade, requires seven hours. One looks with interest at the great St. Bernard Road, over which the Roman army, and the troops of Charlemagne, of Frederic Barbarossa, and Napoleon I. marched. There are places where the carriage seems to hang over the verge of the cliffs, and one considers the possibilities of escape in case of accident. The driver, however, here becomes a leader. One of the horses is taken from the carriage, and the patient fellow walks at the horse's head, carefully leading him down the grade by the bridle.

It rains nearly every day in Switzerland, and the hope that this day would be an exception began to fade away. It looked like rain. The clouds were marshaling their forces. I was without waterproof, but, fortunately, seated in the carriage where I would be protected if it rained. Two ladies, one of whom was from Chicago, and the other a fair young violinist, both from the steamer *City of Chicago*, were on the front seat. Sitting there, they had no protection from the storm. If it rained, I would surely have to be polite, and exchange my seat with them.

It rained. "Ladies, will you be so kind as to come back here, and permit me to ride in the rain?"

It took some courage to say that, but I said it, and felt myself a taller man for being so self-sacrificing.

"O no, sir, thank you! We chose these seats for

better or worse, just as a woman does when she takes a husband. In this case, as often in that, it proves to be for worse, but we propose to abide by our own choice."

Here was the true spirit, and I knew that it would be safe now for me to insist on going out. The ladies wrapped their waterproofs about them, and sat out, while I sat in. When we reached Chamounix, I expressed my gratitude.

"Young ladies, I have five sons!"

"So many! We thought you had sons, and so were kind to you, but we did not dream that you had so many."

"You may have your choice—blonde or brunette."

Then they wanted to know which one was most like his father, supposing that, if they drew him, he would permit them to sit out "till the clouds rolled by."

We had come far to see Mount Blanc. But the mountain was not on exhibition, his person was veiled by impenetrable mists. If we did not see the mountain, we had seen enough to delight us. The glaciers, extending down nearly to the road, could not be hidden, and when first I looked on them, I experienced that indescribable pang which takes hold on the heart like the clutch of an iron hand. It is not surprise, it is not awe, but rather a commingling of the two feelings, producing an emotion, to express which no word has ever been framed. During the night I arose several times and looked out toward the mountain, but the veil was still over it. Each time I retired disappointed. After all I was not to see Mount Blanc. No matter what or how much we enjoy in life, if there be one thing denied us, we fret like spoiled children. We may say "sour grapes" of the good unattained, but we know that they are sweet, and sweeter far because they are beyond our reach.

I fell soundly asleep and dreamed of hidden glory that words could not express, and of visions such as the apostle had, so near us, but between them and us there floated a cloud. The door of my room was opened and I heard a voice:

"Doctor, get up quickly and see Mount Blanc!"

To my delight the clouds were gone, the murky veil had been torn aside, and the queen of mountains shone forth in robes of spotless purity! With a strong glass we looked into the fissures in the glaciers hundreds of feet in depth, where many venturesome travelers have lost their lives. For miles the eternal snows appeared without a wrinkle; then the surface was broken by abrupt precipices, clear and distinct as though cut with a knife. Again, square blocks of glistening ice and snow stood up, shaven down, as it were, on all sides, as definitely as though the mountain's

God had measured them with square and compass. We could, by the telescope, see a party of tourists with ropes attached to their persons binding them together seeking out a way to the summit. A short time afterward I saw that the papers published the account of the loss of a traveler and guide who had been deceived by the new-fallen snow, and stumbled over one of the precipices.

We took our breakfast by a window looking out on the mountain.

Never until my eyes are opened to see no more darkly do I hope for another such vision.

An hour later we took our seats on a char-a-banc and were off for Cluse, where we take the cars for Geneva. I had some difficulty in getting the name of the vehi cle in which we were to travel, but taking up the word in the old spelling-school fashion, I got it at last fixed in my memory; c-h-a-r char-a chara b-a-n-c banc, charabanc. It is an immense omnibus drawn by five horses, and has a seating capacity on the outside for twenty-four persons. Our friends from the hotel came out to see the charabanc, but we insisted that they came simply to see us off. It is never wrong to put the most favorable construction on the conduct of others.

The twenty-seven miles to Cluse is made in four and one-half hours. For an hour we had the glaciers in sight, and then scenery of mountains and valleys, where

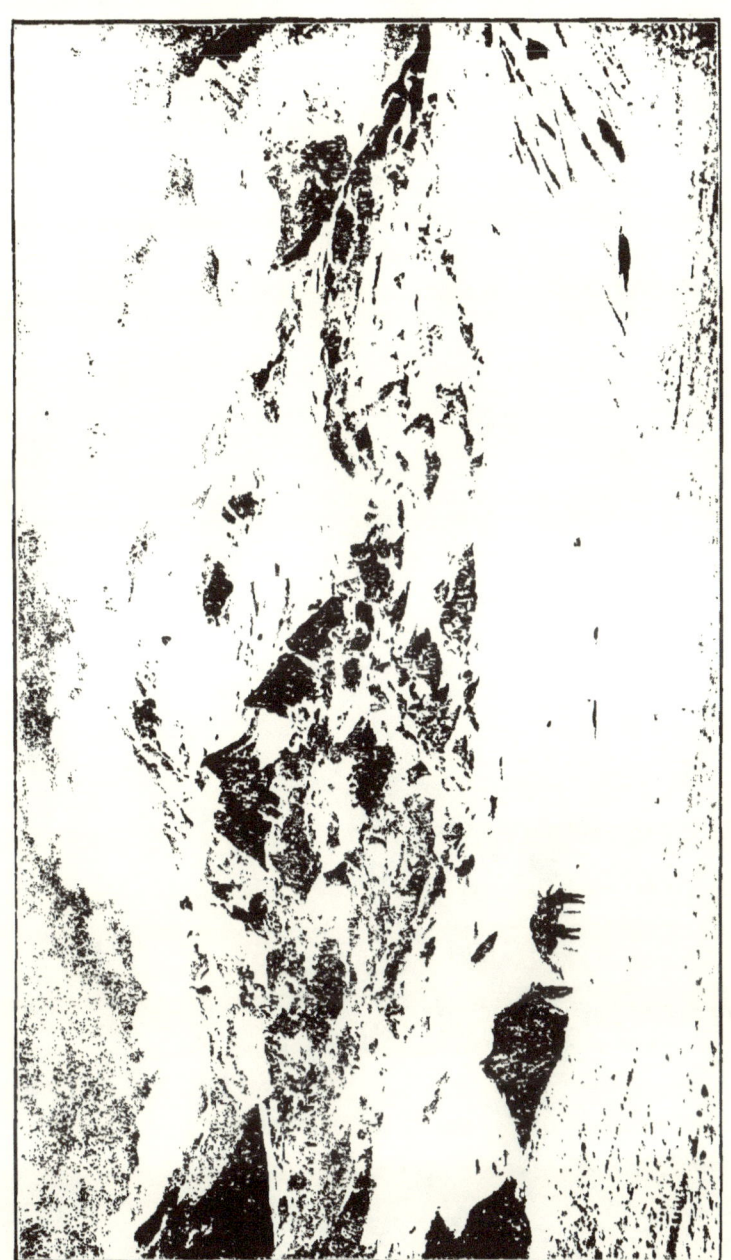

MOUNT BLANC.

the peasants were engaged in bringing in the harvests of wheat and oats. The ride was so restful, that had it not been for fear of a fate similar to that which befell the poor fellow who was present in body when Paul preached a long sermon, I would have fallen asleep.

We passed the village of Saint Gervais, and a friend with a guide-book read that it was "finely situated." It was not finely situated when we saw it. Like many other Swiss villages, it was situated in a narrow valley, and far above it were the mountains with their burdens of snow and ice. One of the glaciers had, for years, and it may be for centuries, been forming and adding to its heavy burdens. The lowest part of the glacier would melt away, and then the ice would sink into the soft earth gradually, but surely, forming an embankment, back of which, in the heat of summer, a great volume of water collected. As each successive year the glacier pressed down farther on this embankment, it became stronger, and was enlarged in extent. The present summer (1892) was unusually warm, and the volume of water became so great, that the embankment could not resist the pressure, but gave way, and was carried down the mountain-side, making a great river of mud. It flooded the town of Saint Gervais, filling the streets, and covering or sweeping away houses, and destroying the lives of twenty-two of the villagers. It was Johnstown on a smaller scale, but the impetus of these waters was even greater than those, and its power was doubled, because it was liquid earth mingled with rocks that smote the doomed village. It was two weeks after this terrible visitation that we passed along the road where the finely situated town had been. Men were at work unearthing the houses, and getting ready to begin life again, in the hope that many years must necessarily elapse before a similar catastrophe could occur.

The peasant can live safely on the mountains during the summer months, and find there good pasture for his cows, but when the winter approaches he comes down to his cottage nearer the plain, and takes his cows into the same house in which he lives. They have different apartments, but are covered by the same roof, and protected by the same walls. Poverty takes away the poetry from the life of the Swiss peasantry. They can not hope to rise above their present condition, and in fact they have but little seeming desire to do more than make a living. In this they are like the peasantry of all Europe.

The Alps are not so rugged as our mountains. There are no such bold chasms as may be seen on the Rio Grande Road. With us the timber line is definitely marked, but in Switzerland there is no special line but that of snow. With us the snow in summer lies in deep gorges, and the bold projections of the mountains are rocks uncovered and dark, while the waters rush down through these gorges into great wide-mouthed canyons, but in Switzerland the whole mountain is covered with snow, and as it melts, the streams find their way directly down the mountain sides, in many places not having worn their course, and leaping from sharp projections, which may in years be worn into gorges. Thus cataracts are formed which bewilder us with their beauty and boldness. The glacier can be formed only where there are two peaks, the ice river forming between them, but a hundred streams may issue from a single mountain slope, whose waters rush to the plain before the winter's rigor comes to bind them to the rocks.

Mount Blanc is 15,730 feet high, but those who are ambitious to ascend the highest mountain in Europe can have their desires gratified at a cost of about fifty dollars in gold, and with some chances of their families realizing on their life-insurance policies at an early date. It is said that the view from the summit is not good, and snow all about you becomes, after awhile, a little monotonous, but then you can have an Alpine stock and get someone to carve on it the words, "Mount Blanc." I felt that I had a right to do this because I had seen the mountain.

Geneva is the largest and most wealthy city of Switzerland. It is celebrated as the home of John Calvin, and also for the manufacture of watches. But there is no place you will go where time is as poorly kept as in Geneva. Chronometers do not agree, and your own timepiece, that has always been right, begins to confuse you by not agreeing with any other watch in the city. The house in which John Calvin lived is shown the visitor, and aside from the fact that the great doctrinarian did much of his labor there, it has no interest whatever. The church in which he preached is in excellent repair, and services are still held in it. The eloquence of Calvin is commented on freely, and his great work in the cause of the reformation will excite the gratitude of those who are willing to honor the truth, no matter to what part of the evangelical church they may be attached. After his return from banishment in 1538, he gained almost absolute power, and this he exercised with undue rigor. But he is not to be judged in the light of our times, and the tyranny of the past may have been no worse than the liberty of the future, if it be turned into licentiousness.

My friend could not forget the treatment of the Spanish physician who was arrested, although not condemned, by the order of Calvin. He insisted on seeing the place where Servetus was burned, but no one seemed to be aware of the fact that the Spanish heretic was treated so warmly by inhospitable Geneva. We may, while condemning intolerance, show so much bitterness that we condemn ourselves for that of which we accuse Calvin. Pretended liberalists sometimes talk so harshly of the defects of Calvin that I am inclined to think they would have shown their hatred of persecution by burning the persecutor, if he were alive. Let us remember that we are more than three centuries away from the struggles of Geneva and rejoice in a system that has done much to give us our religious freedom. While we may neither justify nor yet make apologies for sixteenth-century cruelty, let us be fair enough to judge it and condemn it in the light of the sixteenth, and not of the nineteenth century. The same broad charity that would have saved the life of a sixteenth-century heretic ought to consider well the circumstances of time and place before passing judgment. The work of the great reformer has been established in Geneva and all the vicissitudes of fortune to which the city has been subjected have not been able to destroy that work.

Within a few miles of Geneva, Voltaire lived. One may be a champion of freedom, and yet reject the only foundation stone on which that temple can be erected. The ride to Coppet, of one hour by steamer, to the house of Madame de Staël, and to the chapel in which her body is buried, is taken by many who have read "Corinne," and, with her glowing descriptions in mind, have paid a visit to Italy. The life of this gifted

woman is so full of adventure that one feels tempted
to turn aside from his tour to study it. A melancholy
interest attaches to it. Her mind was gifted, and
her ability to draw pen pictures has seldom been
equaled. The magic of her name, the cruelties to
which she was subjected, the power that she had over
the people, the terror that she inspired in the hearts
of rulers, the generous sympathy she expressed to the
cause of freedom, her associations with the most eminent writers of her time, her idolatry of literary fame,
her weakness in concealing her marriage that she
might not be compelled to give up the name bearing
which she had secured her power, read almost like a
romance, and yet truth is stranger than fiction. Over
her grave is the inscription in Latin: " Here at last
rests one who never rested."

It is strange to see the blue waters of the Rhone
and the muddy, clay-colored waters of the Arve flowing quite a distance in the same channel before they
commingle. It looks as though the pure Rhone were
unwilling to be one with her dishonored sister. Both
streams came from mountain heights; both were born
in the snow, but one has carried more of the defile-
ment of earth with her than the other. Two people
who associate intimately for years with each other
will, after a while, grow into one likeness. Happily
the Arve accepts the blue of the Rhone, and loses

its dull gray. It is thus in life; the stronger nature predominates over the weaker. But the weaker nature may be the best favored, and, as in the vision of the cattle, the lean and ill-favored may devour the fairer ones, and yet remain as poor and hungry and ugly as they were before.

But the city of the great reformer needs to secure a better reputation for honesty. The most outrageous overcharges, for everything, may be expected, and there is but little use in protesting. Make your visits brief.

We left Geneva late in the evening, having secured sleeping-car tickets, for which we paid about twice as much as we would have had to pay in America. We were booked to Paris, and entered the proper car, where we gave up our tickets to the porter, and sought our compartments. Such a sleeping-car, at home, would never be sent out on a second trip. An indignant public would surely "ditch it."

I was growling, in regular Western style, about the stuffy little places where human beings were to be stowed away, when the guards came to the window. They began demanding something, I knew not what. They indicated that there was something wrong, and that it must be made right immediately. A gentleman from Virginia, seated near me, said that they were demanding extra fare from me. I told him to

tell them that if they would give me back the money
I had already paid them, I would settle the matter by
going into the day-coach, which was far more comfortable than the sleeper could possibly be made. He
told me that they refused. I answered, through him,
that they had put me in this compartment; that they
had accepted my tickets; that they refused to return
my money in order to get me out, and that, under
these conditions, I proposed to stay where I was.
The gentleman assured me that the train had already
been detained ten minutes on my account, and that
they could not move it until they had the extra fare.
I said I was not in a hurry. The gentleman said that
his purse was at my disposal. I assured him that
it was not a question of money, but of the rights of
American citizens, and that they might stay there all
night before I would give them any more. Then the
conductor blew his little whistle and the train moved
out. The porter said that he had made the mistake,
and that he would have to lose the money himself.
On hearing this we willingly gave him the extra fare.

Then we began to retire. The doctor had a physician with him in his compartment, and the two of them
got along very comfortably. But there were four in
the one I was placed in—it was not large enough for
two—a gentleman and his sister and an American
student and myself. The gentleman told me that his

sister was seriously embarrassed. He had a lower berth and she an upper. The distance between the two upper berths was about twelve inches, and there were no curtains. I agreed to let him go up and I would remain down. Later on, I heard the lady ask for the curtain. They did not have any curtain. I gave the young student the same caution I have often heard a young mother give a little child when she is impatient for it to go to sleep, and told him that it was cheaper for the company to have the passengers shut their eyes than it was to buy curtains. The car had but one wash-bowl, and it in so small a closet that you had no space for bending over to keep the water from dripping on your person. The charge was in inverse proportion to the accommodations. If I have any friends whose comfort is dear to me, I would say to them, never, under any circumstances, take a sleeper in Europe, unless it be in Germany; and if I had any enemies, and were wicked enough to seek to take their punishment into my own hands, I would put them in a continental sleeper, where, if they did not smother to death before morning, they would certainly feel, when that morning came, that life was not worth living. The student told me that he had met a Chicagoan a few days before, who, when eating black bread and unsalted butter, and drinking muddy coffee, expressed his gratitude by saying, "This is what a man gets for going away from home." Ordinary discomforts are easily forgotten in the pleasures of the morrow; but there has no joy come to my life so intense that I have been able to forget the night in the sleeper between Geneva and Paris. It may be that as I get older the impressions will gradually fade away from my memory, and if so, I will surely regard forgetfulness as one of the blessings of old age.

I have often slept in the open air with my saddle for a pillow, and in feather beds that were so high I had to get on a chair to get in, but never did it fall to my lot to endure such drowsy torture as I experienced that night shutting off half my breathing capacity for the sake of my fellows in the compartment.

CHAPTER X

IT was early in the morning when we arrived at Paris. The first impression was that of an American city, but the cabmen did not seem to be so eager for passengers as with us in America. At the hotel we found some satisfaction in being addressed in well-spoken English. One of our boxes had been expressed from Heidelberg, and I proposed to the doctor that I would take a cab and get the box. He smiled, and said that we were in Paris, and my German would not avail me so much as it did elsewhere, but that if I felt competent to the undertaking, he would be delighted to be alone a little while. I was certain of success. I had a receipt for this box, that measures exactly eighteen by fourteen and one-half inches. Moreover, this receipt was on blue paper, a color that both in war and peace I have discovered to be a sure harbinger of success.

I have a little advice to give the reader. Advice is about the only thing that I am anxious to get rid of in the way of absolute gratuity. It weighs one down when he has it and sees so many people in need of it.

He feels his importance when proffering it and can assume for the moment an air of true benevolence. It may be worth much or little, but that does not figure in the case at all. There is no absolute value fixed on it.

Many years ago a bombastic fellow was walking on a street in Washington, Pennsylvania. He was dressed in Parisian style, and on this particular morning wore a diamond pin, the precious stone being set in such a way as to make it appear several times larger than it really was. He looked down at the jewel with pride, and then up to bow to someone meeting him. Then he looked for the jewel again, and it was gone. There was the pin, with the rough catches that once held the jewel standing up ragged as the molar tooth of an old man who has lived on Florida beef for half a century, and found that while the inside of the tooth gave way, the enamel kept the outside from decay. It became like the outer walls of an extinct diminutive volcano. He began the search for the stone. Others joined him, and for an hour they looked on the sidewalk and in the gutter, but failed to find the object of their search. A little boy came trudging along to school and saw the men all looking to the ground. His bright eyes were bent in the same direction, and in an instant he saw something there of exceeding brilliancy. He stopped and took it in his hand, seeing which the gentleman walked up and claimed it. The little fellow readily gave it up and was turning away, when the generous soul of the stranger rose to the occasion.

"Stop, my dear boy! Stop one moment! How strange, how passing strange it is, that we men should spend an hour in earnest search for this diminutive, bright-eyed creature and fail to find it, when, as by the merest chance, this little boy should come along and pick it up. A thousand thanks, my lad! A thousand thanks, and here are three cents as a reward for your great kindness. A thousand thanks!"

Fewer pennies, and more thanks, would have suited the boy better.

Thanks are like advice, sometimes precious, but never very costly, unless it be to the recipient. My advice is this: If you contemplate a tour of the continent, pick up a little French and German before you leave home, or else pick up a companion who has these useful accomplishments, and then cleave to him as fast as Ruth did to Naomi. I obtained instructions from the porter, and he called a cab and instructed the driver, who only knew that he was taking a stupid American to a certain station, for a certain box, for which the American had a receipt, and that the American was a youth, innocent of all Parisian ways and speech. The driver's duty was to take me to the

10

station, and remain outside until I returned, and then bring me back again.

A new road always seems longer than one with which we are familiar. It was a full half-hour before the cab stopped in front of the station. I went in, and asked at least fifty clerks for someone who spoke English. No answer. At last I stopped in front of a business-looking fellow and spoke. He looked at me as if to say:

"What heathen country are you from, anyway? And how do you expect me to understand a language that may be used only by cannibals?"

Then I took out my large receipt.

He looked at it, and then at the ceiling.

I wondered if he thought, from the size and color of the paper, that I was after the job of papering the office. He saw that it was written over. Then he looked at it more carefully, and wiped his spectacles, and looked at me.

He took me to a second man, who looked at the receipt, and then at me. Not a word was spoken.

He took me to a third man, who guessed at the meaning of the receipt, and looked over a large file of papers, which I supposed were duplicate receipts. I was happy now, for this man evidently knew what he was doing. But he handed me back the paper, saying something in French, and if he knew what he

was doing, I had at least the consolation of not knowing what he was saying.

It is well for some of us that we do not know what
people are saying about us; but when a man is speaking to us, it is better for us to know what he says. A
happy thought struck me. It is possible for people to
write so that we can understand them. The pronunciation is what is wrong with the French language. I
handed him a pencil and piece of paper, and he wrote,
in plain words, "*du Nord.*" I went out to my
coachman, feeling now that I would soon be a French
scholar, and said, "*du Nord.*" The coachman smiled,
and motioned for me to get in. He started at a rapid
rate for "*du Nord.*" Here I went through the same
operation as before, and looked over a pile of boxes,
but failed to see ours.

The clerk said: "*Gare de l'Est.*"

I suddenly lost all my linguistic pride. Pride goeth
before destruction. I would have willingly confessed that I knew nothing of French—or even German, that I understood but little English, if it would
have relieved me from my perplexity. I forgot all
about the use of the pencil, which had helped me in
the last station. He repeated the words that perplexed
me. There seemed to be something about a garden,
and about some sort of delay. Then a happy thought

came to me : I will try if they do not speak German, and began :

"*Sprechen sie Deutch?*"

Not one of the clerks spoke German. The situation was becoming alarming. The clerks were losing their patience. It was a losing game all around, except that the coachman was counting the hours. He was happy as he saw added to the usual charge for a trip to the station hours of time and more francs.

I had determined not to return to the hotel without the box, and give the doctor an opportunity to ask me why I did not try "Dutch" with him, and add that these French people all understand the pure German readily.

A lady came in walking with a younger lady, who resembled her so much that I saw the relationship of mother and daughter. They saw my perplexity. They turned and began talking to the clerk in French. "I never heard as ugly a language in my life as the French," I thought to myself. The lady smiled and said "America." I took courage. She turned and addressed me in a pitying sort of way and said, "*Gare de l'Est.*"

I was to be mocked with those words all the time. What had I done that I should be tortured so? Was I being punished for talking German to the professor?

The lady smiled at my confusion, and I bowed most profoundly and said:

"Pardon me, but does Madame speak English ?"

"O, yes, quite readily," she answered in as sweet, plain-spoken words as you ever heard. How interesting she became. I was willing to be entertained by anyone that spoke my mother tongue. She was evidently a lady, and, regarding the proprieties of the occasion, asked promptly:

"What will Monsieur have ?"

"I would have Madame talk," I replied, believing that it would not offend her so much if I slightly varied the usual order of our words.

Again she laughed and said: "The easiest thing in the world for a woman to do. But what would you have me say ?"

"Honor me by saying in English what he is trying to tell me in French."

"He says that your trunk is not here, and that it is probable you may find it at the East Station." She kindly wrote the words for me on a slip of paper, and I, more humble now, showed the paper to the coachman, in place of attempting to pronounce the words. In about twenty minutes he landed me at the " *Gare l'Est.*" Here, again, I had my usual experience. It seemed now as though it were the proper thing to have. If you asked a man if he spoke English, the right thing for him to do was to stare at you and make no reply. But I had a lexicon in my pocket that I had not used. It is more than a lexicon; it is something that talks. Money talks in Paris. It is a language that all Europe understands. The larger the coin, the clearer the speech. I made an eloquent address to one of the clerks. He was the first man that understood me thoroughly. He put what I said in his pocket, and led me to another room, where I presented my receipt. The clerk there looked over it and spoke to me in French. He called up a man who spoke in German. He told me that there were eight francs to pay. I paid them. He then began a series of questions which I managed to answer to his satisfaction. How I wished that the doctor had been about, to hear me talk German! Then he gave me a paper to sign. I did not know what the paper was, but I signed it. Then he fired a whole volley of questions at me, which I meekly answered.

" Who are you ? "

" Where do you live ? "

"When did you leave home ? "

" What did you leave home for ? "

" What is your business in life ? "

" When did you go to Germany ? "

" What were you doing in Germany ? "

"Where did you go to from Germany ? "

" When did you come to Paris ? "

" Where are you stopping in Paris ? "

" Why did you come to Paris? "

" How long will you stay in Paris ? "

" Where will you go from Paris ? "

" What have you in your box ? "

Then he gave me a paper as large as my receipt, and pointed to another window. There I was given another paper to sign. I signed it. Then they gave me my receipt and pointed to another room. I obeyed, and found myself in the presence of a few custom-house officials, and many strangers, and a huge pile of boxes. I was glad to see the clerk whom I had paid for services before, in this room. He motioned for me to look up my box. I succeeded in finding it, when the fellow pulled it out of the pile, and left it and me together. In a few minutes an officer touched me and directed with his hand the way to the room I had just come from. Here a German-speaking officer wanted to know why my name was not Davis. I told him because it was Meloy. Doctor Davis' name was on the box. He had signed the receipt as owner. This involved another talk, and more explanations. The officials were satisfied, however, and sent me to my box. I opened it, and stood by it.

I was not so lonesome as I had been.

There were the soiled linen, and wooden shoes, and

other valuables that belonged to us. At last two men came along and began to unpack the box for me. They opened collar boxes, and peered inside the "Dutch" shoes, and ran their dirty hands over shirt fronts, crumpled up our dress suits, and then pasted a tab on the lid and tried to shut it down.

It would not shut.

So they pounded down on the contents with both hands, like a woman kneading bread, until the lid was closed. I motioned a porter to take it out now, but he simply shook his head. After half an hour, during which time I stood by the box thinking, he came and handed me a paper, and taking the box on his shoulder, loaded it on the coach. Then he took a half-franc from me, and gave a ticket to the driver and one to me. The cabman started, only to be stopped by a guard who took the tickets from us, and we were off for the hotel. I had been three hours getting through the custom house. The doctor had given me up as lost, and to his anxious inquiries I replied:

"I have been talking German to a man at the station!"

Then he said: "I wish you had been lost!"

I have not overdrawn this experience in the least, but I have since found out that all persons coming from Germany or sending goods from Germany to France have trouble. France suspects every man and everything that comes from Germany. Had my trunk not been sent from Heidelberg, or had I not been able to speak German at all, I would have fared better. "A little learning is a dangerous thing." The hatred of France and Germany is apparent. It runs through all classes of people. These nations are preparing for war, and sooner or later it will come. The French people are not only biding their time, but are preparing to regain Alsace and Lorraine.

Germany is increasing her army in expectancy of a struggle, and hence it is that the women must work while the men play soldier. It is the misfortune of both countries that in the hour of victory a most ungenerous policy was pursued toward the vanquished. Germany points to the ruins left by the victorious French, and France, remembering the insults to her flag, and the capture of her provinces, says, with exceeding bitterness, "Revenge!"

You can not pass through these countries without having your sympathies awakened on one side or the other. Had there only been a Grant commanding the German army when Paris was captured, there would have been good feeling and lasting peace between the two great nations.

"Keep your horses," said the hero of Vicksburg when Richmond fell; "you will need them for the spring plowing!"

Germany did not pursue this policy, and the result is a constant dread of, and preparation for war with the old foe.

But the position of England troubles France. England is friendly to Germany, and her intervention must be prevented, and therefore France is looking toward Russia to say, when the hour comes, " Hands off! " With Russia to keep England quiet, the young and vigorous republic may be able to take the German throat and say, " Give us back Alsace and Lorraine! " These provinces are chafing under the German control, and with an ardent love for their country they sing their songs in captivity with as much of loyalty as ever Israel had when she refused to sing, at the order of her rude captors, " By the Rivers of Babylon."

Just now this feeling is being fanned in Paris by a great *fête* in the Garden of the Tuilleries, which is held to raise funds for the poor of the French and Russian armies. You will see everywhere the letters " F. R.," but occasionally the little character " & " is inserted, so that the people, in place of reading " French Republic, " read " France & Russia."

What the result may be, no one can surely predict. Had there been no changes made in methods of warfare, Germany would have an easy victory in such a conflict; but, under present conditions, where celerity and skill are more to be depended on than mere force and numbers, the result may be very different from what we would naturally expect. It will be a battle between the swift and the strong.

Paris is a beautiful city, whether seen by day or night. A guide is not an absolute necessity. You will learn more by personal observation than you will by having teachers to solve every difficulty for you as soon as it arises. It was with this feeling that we determined to see what we wanted to see in Paris alone. The first place that we went was to the "*Champs Elysées.*" We must begin at once to pronounce names properly and to call the streets "rues."

Champs Elysées—Shauns-a-lee-say, if you please— is sought. The coachman knows at once where you want to go and what you want to see when you say to him, "Champs Elysées." This is the finest part of Paris and is esteemed unequaled in the world. It is a wide avenue, along the sides of which there are pleasure grounds of exceeding beauty. You enter this place of delights by the *Place de la Concorde*, and leave it at the western extremity by the *Arc de Triomphe.* The distance is but one mile, but one mile of unsurpassed beauty. The wide street is filled with carriages and horses splendidly equipped. The avenue leads you through a bewildering scene of lovely promenades and cool, shaded walks, through flower gardens, by sparkling fountains, where tens of thousands meet.

The scene so rich by day is even more imposing by night. Thousands of lamps of colored glass give the impression of varied beauty such as one not often sees; music adds its enchantments, and the open pleasure gardens bid you enter where concerts are held. The words " *entre libre* " have beguiled many a one to take a seat, in the belief that he is for once in his life to have a free show. But he is expected to buy something to eat or drink, and a simple glass of lemonade includes the full price of an admission.

The concert which we attended was, so far as dress and general conduct are concerned, entirely unobjectionable. Young Parisian damsels, modestly attired, sang sweet songs, and young men gave recitations which looked amusing. Polite as Parisians are, they do not deem it discourteous to talk and laugh while someone is entertaining them, unless his entertainment is more fascinating than their conversation. The city throngs these grounds, not to engage in vulgar rioting, but in quest of pleasures that certainly are not debasing.

The credit of founding this beautiful pleasure garden is given to Louis XIV. Some, however, have given the honor to Marie de' Medici, and fix the date at 1616. The avenue itself had been laid out by Marie de' Medici in that year. It seems wonderful to one accustomed to call that old which dates back half a century, to see the beautiful garden substantially as it was two and one-half centuries ago.

The *Bois de Boulogne* is half a mile beyond the *Arc de Triomphe*, which the reader will remember is at the western end of the *Champs Elysées*. The pronunciation here must be learned, or your coachman will not have any idea what you mean. You will find it convenient to say to him, Bwa-deh-boo-lone. Even this place is historic. It is a forest containing twenty-five hundred acres. It has been partially destroyed several times, so that guns might be trained against invading armies. Wellington encamped here, and as late as 1870 the Prussians would have used it when attacking the city; and proud as Paris was of her forest, it was cut down. The trees in it are therefore mostly small, and the drive through it is lacking in interest. The grounds were dusty and the trees parched up with the heat. Much of the beauty of any park depends on rain, and this had not been given to the forest of Paris for some weeks.

In the evening we attended the *fête* in the garden of the Tuilleries. The garden is much larger than it was when the palace was standing. The site of the buildings has been added to the original gardens. The *fête* was to raise funds for the Russian and French armies. As stated before, it was an interesting place to visit. Lamps, of many colors, on hundreds of arches, burned during the evening. Altogether there must have been thousands of these lamps, and they were arranged in so many different forms that it seemed as though special artists had been engaged to put them in place. The lamps were simply little cups filled with some oily substance in which were dipped wicks that burned down to the surface of the oil. Inside this inclosure there were fireworks, merry-go-rounds, toboggan cars, shows, acrobatic performances, concerts, and various kinds of games to attract a penny from the patron.

One fellow interested me. He had a maul in his hands and was bantering passers-by to come and make a trial of their strength with him. A tube stood about fifteen feet high, and in this tube, resting on a spring, was the figure of a handsome lady. If the man had sufficient muscle to give a blow of a certain force, the female figure sprang to the top of the tube and bowed; but if he was not able to strike hard enough, she refused to appear.

In some respects the great *fête* was not unlike a country fair, and within the gates the populace gathered by tens of thousands to enjoy the amusements that were afforded them. How different the scene presented here from what has so often been witnessed on this very ground! The shout of the warrior was heard here; the ground was red with blood; it was covered with the wounded and the dying; victims by the hundred perished here by the blade of the guillotine. Here, too, royalty once reigned and deemed itself secure; here, amid horrors which no pen can ever picture, the Commune went down, and in due time the reign of law and order was established. But it was during the dark days of communistic reign in Paris, between the 18th of March and the 27th of May, 1871, that the most terrible scenes ever enacted in human history occurred. "Then it was," says Victor Hugo, "that Paris was nailed upon the cross for the sins of the whole world." But if we carry out this figure, the Golgotha was the garden of the Tuilleries.

In no other place do we come in such close contact with the struggles of earth. In no other city did the fire-engines throw streams of petroleum to drench buildings that were to be burned. Can it be possible that these gay gardens ever witnessed such horrid cruelties? I recall a little sad history. It dates to this very month of August, and to this very day— August 24, 1572. The houses of Catholics were illuminated that night, not only to designate their location, but to aid in the work of blood, as the cruel orders that came from the heart of the guilty and crafty and venomous Catherine de' Medici were executed. Let us turn away from the scene of all this gaiety, for the blood-red lamps, in the light of which the thoughtless peoples chatter, remind me too much of the blood of thousands who were slain by the hands of cruelty in this vicinity.

It was late Saturday night when we reached the hotel, and there came up in my mind a hundred half-forgotten facts of history, mingled with the memory of the gay crowds that were assembled in the garden, and I wondered why it is that the progress of the nations to a higher form of political freedom has so often been marked by blood. May it not be that the crimson garments have been rolled up forever by the angels of peace, and the sway of Him will soon come of the increase of whose government and peace there shall be no end? It seems as though in Paris I can realize a day of unclouded glory rising after the dark night—a day in which the songs of good-will and fraternity shall be heard after the night whose darkness was pierced by the light of the torch in incendiary hands, and whose hours that should have been still were disturbed by the cries of the terror-stricken and the dying.

There is already a mighty transformation wrought in this wonderful city, and the wish of my heart is expressed in the words that you will so often see on halls and monuments, and that are so often heard as the children express their love and loyalty, "*Vive la République!*"

CHAPTER XI

HE little American church was well filled on Sabbath morning, and a sermon full of good thought was preached. In the evening we sought out the McAll mission, and to our surprise found some two dozen strangers trying to get in. At last, when the number waiting outside had considerably increased, we were told that there was to be no service there that evening, on account of the extreme heat. Our enthusiasm for the mission and our hopes of its success went down together.

Paris is a notoriously Roman Catholic city. If any one had doubts of this before, he would have been fully persuaded on Monday, which was Assumption Day, and is kept by the church. Four-fifths of the stores were closed, either because the proprietors were Catholics, or because they did not want to antagonize the feelings of so many of their own citizens. And yet I noticed that places of entertainment were open as usual.

Paris is no worse than Chicago. Sabbath in America is as much profaned as the Parisian Sunday. There were grave hints of immoral performances which might be seen, but I had not the least desire to look on the darkest side of human depravity, where the sight would be productive of no possible good. Nor could I say that Paris by day, or in the early evening, is a city given to drunkenness. Nearly all Paris drinks. The wines are light and the men and women who imbibe are able to stand up after taking them; but it does not follow that no evil is done. The moral sense may be corrupted and the spiritual life sullied where there has been no bestial intoxication. The effects of this moderate drinking may be seen at a later hour and in the lowest parts of the city. When respectability has put out the lights and retired to rest, the young and old, who once quaffed lighter wines, begin their hateful revels, and down the dark lanes and rows sin holds high carnival, and hell demands her impure orgies. It is an unwilling comment that I make on the habits of many Americans who visit the East, that they fall so readily into the customs of the people. No high standard of morality is maintained, and the youth who accompany the parents, go home to live as their parents did in Europe. Even ministers of the gospel, who have been sent abroad, followed by the prayers of their people, have been known to acquire habits while away which have destroyed their subsequent usefulness, and blighted their whole lives.

The great Vendome column is easily recognized by the pictures of it that have been scattered throughout the world. It was erected by Napoleon I. in 1806, as a monument to his greatness and the bravery of the French army in the wars against Prussia. This column stands in the Place Vendome, and is one hundred and forty-four feet high. The heart of the column is of masonry, and the outside is a series of bronze plates, representing different battle scenes. There are nine hundred feet of these reliefs, and the visitor will never have sufficient time to study them all. To make the column more impressive, it was, in part, constructed of captured cannon, and twelve hundred of these were used for this purpose. On the top of this column was a statue of Napoleon I.

Here, in 1871, the fury of the mob was exhibited. The Commune looked on this as a monument to the triumphs of royalty, and determined to destroy it.

A most interesting description of their efforts in this direction is found in a valuable work, by my gifted friend, Mr. John McGovern, *"The Empire of Information."* "The ceremony of pulling down the Column Vendome was announced for Monday after-noon. The crowd to witness this act of official vandalism was very great. The widest diversity of apprehension was felt as to the result of the shock in falling of the enormous mass of metal and brick. Some thought the street would be crushed through to the sewers. Others believed that all the loaded balconies of the neighborhood would fall. Again, others dreaded seeing the old houses in the vicinity topple and go to pieces. An enormous mass of manure, sawdust, and sand, had been prepared as a bed for the fallen monument, and the ordinary apparatus for moving a house was fixed in the street, a block or so away. The rope from the capstan led to the top of the column. The base had been greatly weakened. The final act was delayed by the operations of two men, at the summit of the monument, trying to fasten the flag of France in the hands of the bronze figure. The tri-color, after many attempts of the men, was fixed in place, and the populace at once perceived that the Commune would be satisfied with nothing short of this insult to the glorious banner of their country. Just as the word was to be given for the closing operation a wind sprang up, and detached the flag from the hand of the bronze Napoleon. The hour was late. The flag must be insulted. The ceremony was postponed until the next day. The following day other things happened to hinder the outrage against art and history, but the people now began to revile the leaders of the Commune for their failure.

This led to redoubled energy, and just before dark, as
the jeering crowd began to adjourn, in contempt of
the unscientific destructiveness of the Commune, the
column was seen to totter. It fell a moment afterward, and the emblem of France's empire over
nearly the whole world was no more."

But when the banner of France fell in the heap of
filth, a shudder of indignation ran through the hearts
of many thousands, that presaged the end of the mad
Commune. The column has since been replaced, and
is regarded with a feeling akin to veneration by the
people, and with abiding interest by the stranger.
But let us away, where we may not hear the story of
blood, if such a place can be found in Paris. We will
go to the *Jardin des Plantes*, and there get rid of the
records of war. But the attempt is vain. In this
wonderful garden, where you find galleries of geology,
and botany, and anatomy, you will also find a vast
menagerie. While you go from one part of this to
another, you are reminded of the days of the siege,
and of the fact that many of the animals of the garden
were eaten by the people to satisfy their hunger.

Where, then, shall we go? The church is a sanctu-
ary and was once a refuge. The blood that is spoken
of there ought to be the blood of sacrifice alone. Near
our hotel is Saint Roch's. It is not a pretentious
building, but services are being held in it. The music

is the finest in Paris. I entered and listened for a while to the music, and presume that it was as represented, but there are degrees in this art so far beyond me that I fail to recognize their excellence.

What of Saint Roch's? In front of this church, a century ago, Napoleon planted his cannon to preserve the peace of the city. It is located on the *Rue St. Honoré*, and surely there is no place in the world where strife has been more determined.

I hasten to the church of the Madeleine. There is something in the name that tells of mercy and pardon. This church is modeled after the Parthenon, at Athens. It is fifty-four feet in height, three hundred and fifty feet long and one hundred and forty feet wide. No services are being held here, but workmen are busy putting an effigy in place, and others erecting a statue of some saint. It is a place frequented by all strangers. A great flight of stone steps leads up to the front entrance. These steps extend nearly the entire width of the building. Here, at last, I have gotten away from the sad sacrifices that man made of his brother! But it must have been near this that the fierce struggles of the Commune raged. The church is near the *Place de la Concorde.* Within these walls three hundred men, who had fled before the army of France, took refuge. These aisles, where so many Catholic knees have bent, were crimsoned with the blood of the fugitives. They came with red hands to the church for refuge, and not one of them escaped. A citizen had revealed their hiding place. The great stone steps were burdened with the dying. It is not a figure of speech, but a truth of history, that the streets of Paris were red with the blood of the slain.

It is not my purpose to write a history of this crime against history, and against humanity, but there is something, in view of the present tendency to secularism in our own country, that will be of particular interest, and to this my attention has been directed by reading the excellent work quoted from a little while ago. It refers to the calendar adopted by the French in 1793. The years and months were to be divided on " philosophical principles." The Christian Era was to be abolished, and the date of reckoning was to be from the formation of the Republic, dating at the time of the autumnal equinox—September 22, 1792. The seasons were to be autumn, winter, spring, and summer. The first month of each period was called Vindemaire, or the month of vintage ; Nivose, or the month of snow ; Germinal, or the month of buds, and Messidor, the harvest month. Each tenth day was to be a day of rest, and the Sabbath was to be forever obliterated. The attempt of France to do away with the institutions of Divine appointment ought to serve as a warning to the Republic of America.

Notre Dame in many respects disappointed me. It was founded in 1163, where once a temple to Jupiter stood. The cultured idolatry of its worship is a step in advance of the services that were rendered in the heathen temple, but there are many longer strides to be taken before its services will conform to the simplicity of New Testament worship. For a consideration, you will be shown a thorn, which, it is claimed, was taken from the crown worn by the Savior, and also a piece of the cross to which he was nailed. I suppose that it would be difficult to prove that these are not what they are represented to be, and even harder to establish the claim that they are. But they are held in high veneration, and if one have sufficient credulity they will do him quite as much good as though their genuineness were fully established. But I am too much of a doubter to enjoy relics that may have so many rivals in the field. The old plum tree in New York City that marked the corner of the Bowery affords an illustration of what I mean. Pieces of the original tree are shown along the North River so numerously that the tree must have been immense, and furnished tons of plums, and several cords of wood.

The interior is filled partly with the statues of kings and saints, and pictures of judgment, in which I take not the least interest. But the windows are worth studying, at least in an artistic way.

The great rose window, forty-two feet in diameter, is the handsomest work I have ever seen ; and if you will get a view of this from the farther end of the cathedral it will be a picture that will always live in memory.

But of all cathedrals that I have seen, *Sainte Chapelle* is the fairest. It dates to about the middle of the thirteenth century, and was built to hold the relics brought back by the Crusaders from Palestine. Its architecture is very peculiar, being narrow in proportion to its length and height. It is one hundred and fifteen feet long, thirty-nine feet wide, and one hundred and fifteen feet high. Its windows, which occupy the greater part of the sides of the structure, are forty-eight feet high, and are of richly-colored glass. The structure is regarded, and I think rightly, as the finest specimen of Gothic art to be found anywhere in France. There are no gloomy walls, and dull pictures, and heavy columns, to oppress you, but all is light and inviting as a crystal palace could be, yet without any glare to dazzle and bewilder. High, slender columns, with their delicate capitals, support graceful arches above you. When I had seen this splendid structure, I did not care to look at any other in France, preferring that this last impression should be left me as that which is unrivaled in church architecture.

What is now the Pantheon was originally the church of Saint Genevieve, erected in the sixth century. It was, however, neglected, notwithstanding the fact that it was built over the bones of Saint Genevieve, the protectress of Paris. Madame de Pompadour set her heart on rebuilding it, and Louis XV. laid the corner stone in 1764. It occupies a commanding position, and now wholly given over to secularism, is a curiosity.

A look at the dome will please you, but it must be taken at the expense of one's neck, for there are no appliances of mirrors or lounges to enable you to look up without some difficulty. It was decorated by Gros, and represents kings of France doing homage to Genevieve. Two hundred and fifty columns are in and around the building. We visited the vaults underneath, not to see where the bodies of Marat and Mirabeau had been, but to look on the casket that once contained the body of Victor Hugo, and to see his sarcophagus. It was a surprise, but one that gave me great pleasure, to notice fastened to one of the silver handles of the casket a small silk flag—the stars and stripes. In this building the Commune had placed powder, intending to add to their other acts of vandalism the destruction of the Pantheon, but the army prevented the execution of the plot.

It is a fitting place for the ashes of Hugo to rest. He was a patriot in sympathy with the Commune's desire to fight the enemies of France, yet opposing the madness of the mob. No pen was ever held in human hands that had more wonderful powers of description than his. It is proper that if cathedrals are to be cemeteries, they should at least not have within their vaults the bodies of men who were not noted for their piety or grace.

We leave the Pantheon and are driven to the *Dome des Invalides*, where is the tomb of the great Napoleon. Napoleon died in exile, May 5, 1821. The body was brought to Paris by the way of the *Bois de Boulogne*, beneath the Arch of Triumph, and to its present resting place, December 15, 1840.

The red granite sarcophagus weighs sixty-seven tons, and cost two thousand eight hundred dollars. Around this sarcophagus are statues of victory, and in the mosaic pavement a beautiful wreath. Above the door of the crypt is a sentence taken from his will:

Je désire que mes cendres reposent sur les bords de la Seine au milieu de ce peuple Français que j'ai taut aimé.

"I desire that my ashes may repose upon the banks of the Seine, in the midst of the French people, whom I have ever loved."

The words have a sad sort of melody in them, especially when we remember that he was by birth a Corsican, and that his heart had been broken by banishment, as the waves were broken on the rocks of

Saint Helena. But the sorrows of his exile had softened his nature.

The Garden of the Luxembourg was a disappointment. It may have been so because we visited it in the dry season of the year. It was early in August, but the lawns were without greenness, and that is to be without beauty. We strolled under trees which had been robbed of their foliage by the drought. We walked along paths where the dead leaves had not been swept up. An American forest, burning with gold when the frosts have touched it, is even fairer than the rich verdure of the early spring-time; but, Oh, the dreariness of a park with dead leaves all about you! The flower garden was inviting, yet it showed the effects of hot and dry weather. Near it is the place where many of the communists were executed in 1871.

How thankful I was that the attempt to burn the Louvre was a failure! It is the most interesting place in Paris, if not in the world. As we pass through its galleries, devoted to art, it is hard for us to realize that these very halls (in the older part) were the residences of royalty, and that in them there was the most fiendish plot devised that ever came to a cruel nature. It is enough to say that the palace was occupied by Catherine de' Medici, and her son, Charles IX., who but too willingly obeyed the mandates of his wicked mother. It was from this palace that the order was given for the massacre of Saint Bartholomew's. But a little distance away is the church from the tower of which the signal bell was rung. This palace, and that of the Tuilleries, occupied twenty-four acres. Royalty needed room to breathe. And yet, so infatuated were the rulers of France with their brief authority, that they must also have palaces at Versailles.

CHAPTER XII

THE Louvre is given up to art, and who that has stood before the sweet sculptured face of "Venus de Milo," or examined the wonders of the brush in the hands of masters in their art, could suggest a better purpose to which the palaces of kings could be put? There is a gem room in the Louvre which all who have but limited time ought to inspect with greatest care. It will do to wander through the other parts of the building, where there is enough to engage your attention for years, had you the time, but in this small room you surely may spend many hours with profit and delight.

It is interesting to study the art of Fra Angelica, who knew nothing whatever of perspective, and whose paintings are as flat as blue and white dinner plates; but if the soul is to be enlarged, it must be in studies of more recent works. In this room, *Salon Carre*, are clustered together the gems of the Louvre. A single painting of Murillo, which some conceited fellow was ostentatiously copying (?), was purchased in 1852 at a cost of $120,000.

The great artists had their weaknesses and attempted to immortalize themselves by painting their own portraits among the figures of the scene. It must be said, however, that they did not always give their features to the one performing the most exalted service, as in the "Marriage at Cana," by Paul Veronese. The artist made exact portraits of his fellows, and gave them all places in the orchestra. Titian has a bass-viol; Bassano holds a flute; Paul Veronese, dressed in white, has a viol; and Tintoretto also holds a viol.

I always supposed that the author somehow managed to get himself in his book, but was ignorant of the fact that the artist actually produced his own likeness on the canvas. How hard it is for us to get away from ourselves! We reap what we have sown, but the harvest we gather in, like the reaper, has grown into the likeness of the seed.

Yet, who was Paul Veronese? His very name is obscured by his greatness. His name was Cagliari. But he became such a universal favorite that he took the name of the city in which he was born, Verona, and was known as Paul Veronese. The honor totally obscured the man, and not one in a thousand who looks on his works has the least conception of his true name. His pictures are full of what in literature would be anachronisms, and he seemed to delight in doing violence to the proprieties of time and country.

But his greatness is seen in the fact that his works rose superior to his errors.

Rubens must have been an artless man, while a model artist. It is sometimes esteemed a weakness for a man to talk much of his wife, in the belief that her noble qualities will speak for themselves, and it is specially esteemed indelicate for him to talk much of his first wife in the presence of his second. Rubens talked in his pictures of his first wife, utterly regardless of the criticisms of the world, and of his second wife. Her fair face and red mantle appear in every painting where it is possible to bring forth a noble character. This appears much nobler than the work of the artist, Palma the Younger, who paints the judgment scene, and among those on the left hand, who are being consigned to their terrible doom, is to be found the picture of his wife. How a man could mingle fine colors, who had such an unrefined nature, it is difficult to tell. "One may smile and be a villain," and I suppose that one may paint without being desperately in love with his wife; but we may rightly expect nothing very refined from a coarse nature.

I have also been surprised at the work that these artists have done, as to its quantity as well as quality. It is said that they worked for eternity, and if so, they surely were not idlers. How could one man do so much? To Rubens there are ascribed eighteen hundred paintings, many of them large. It has been estimated that every week in which he was engaged in his art he must have produced a picture. But it is probable that many of them were made by others under his direction. Admitting this, every one of them bears the stamp of his genius.

The orator gives out with every sentence he utters something of his life to his hearers, and the artist gives something of his life to the canvas. Every touch of the brush has in it a fine frenzy, a loving ardor, a glowing devotion, that must, like a burning flame, consume the life. The artist obtained promotion; he secured the crown; he lives in the conceptions of his brain, and the work of his hand, but he paid the full price, and paid it in advance. Shall the one who speaks to the soul by the harmony of eternal truth have less zeal and more of murmuring than they had who spoke through the colors and shadings made by the brush?

Art ennobles, and nature gives rest, only where there is truth. Pictures may tell the most egregious lies, and a cartoon may be guilty of the basest slanders. It is no wonder that the wise critic should advise his friend to "utter nothing regardlessly," but that friend spoke through pictures.

Versailles is only ten miles by rail from Paris. The booking agent is a lady, who no doubt speaks beautiful

12

French, but not a word of English. I had, however, learned the universal language of pantomime to such perfection that one would have mistaken me for a mute.

One evening, for example, an Italian peasant girl entered our compartment, carrying a pet chicken. I told the doctor that I proposed having a talk with her about her chicken. The doctor looked reprovingly at me. He expected that I would insist on using my favorite German. His rebuke only made me more determined in my attempt; so I began by laying down my thumb near the chicken's head, and then, making an imaginary axe of my hand, struck the thumb a blow; that was the first act. The second was to go through the process of picking the feathers from an imaginary chicken, and after this, and the singeing process, and the potting of the fowl, I represented the act of eating. It took a good while to act it all out, and would be rather an expensive way of talking, if time were of any value. It is easy when you have done this to turn the head just a little to one side, with a sort of inquisitive jerk, and you have the question. She guessed my charade at once, and, taking the chicken to her arms, shook her head, and stroked the feathered fowl very tenderly. Then she answered, in words, as much as to say, "I know by your looks that you are a preacher, and fond of fowl, but no clergyman shall ever eat my chicken." She held it in her arms after that, as closely as a mother would her child in the presence of a cannibal.

How will I buy tickets from an agent to Versailles? The agent does not care to have you act out a long charade, in order to sell a ten-mile ticket. I had learned to pronounce the name "*Versi.*"

I held up two fingers and said, "*Versi!*" then threw down some money, making sure that it was enough.

She asked me something, which may have been how old I was, but I guessed (all Americans say, "I guess")—no matter, "I guessed" this time that she wanted to know about a return ticket. I shook my head, which is the universal language for "No, I thank you." Then we climbed to the top of an observation car and were off.

Versailles was only a hunting ground in the time of Louis XIII. It was, however, enlarged and made palatial, and became the royal residence during the reign of Louis XIV., who built another palace, some distance from the first one, which he called the Grand Trianon. Louis XV. built, near this, another smaller palace, called the *Petit Trianon.* These several palaces were occupied by the crown until the time of the revolution.

I used to think that a nation that was cursed with a king had only to keep up one palace; but **a** small

kingdom may have a dozen palaces, or even more ; and
the visits of the king or queen to these palaces is
remembered as a notable event in history. If I had not
seen any other palaces, I would by these alone have
been reminded of the warning that the patriot of Israel
gave to the people when they proposed taking on airs
so as to be like the nations about them. It may suit
the ideas of people who want to live like their neighbors to have royal rulers, but it involves a large payment for the luxury. People are willing, even in
America, to pay for the honors that someone else may
carry. These palaces, however, have in France been
turned into splendid national museums. The number
and extent of them can hardly be realized by one who
has not gone through the greater and smaller galleries.
The large palace at Versailles has in it one hundred
and nine rooms devoted now to art.

Looking from the windows of this palace, the view
is one that bewilders you with the vastness of the gardens, where you may see flowers blooming by the banks
of artificial lakes, evergreens trimmed in different
shapes, and many pieces of statuary. Here are fountains that used to play at an expense of two thousand
dollars a day. They are not often active now, but
royalty did not care for the cost, just so that it might
be entertained.

The rooms of the great palace are filled with costly

paintings, representing the glory of the French arms. The figure of Napoleon I. is everywhere present. The thrill of pleasure that I experienced in visiting the Pantheon is redoubled here, as I look on portraits of Washington and LaFayette. We do not forget the name that is thus closely associated with that of Washington, and recall once more the visit of LaFayette. with his young son, George Washington LaFayette, to America, who, when he saw the sarcophagus at Mount Vernon, fell on his knees and kissed it. The memory of the services of France to the cause of our liberty endears the French people to us.

The Grand Trianon is one mile from Versailles, and was erected by Louis XIV. as a sort of quiet resting place. But uneasy rests the head that wears a crown, and the King soon grew weary of it. As you have seen the palace at Versailles, you realize that this one was not needed. But now, certainly, having been at the Louvre and this palace, you have exhausted the art treasures of France. Enter the Trianon and be taught a new lesson, as you pass through salôns, and dining-rooms, and circular salôns, and grand galleries, and library-rooms, and billiard-rooms, and sleeping-rooms, and private rooms, and reception-rooms, and vestibules, the walls of which are covered with famous paintings, and the ceilings ornamented at a fabulous outlay of time and genius and money. At last you are glad to get out and breathe the pure air of heaven, under a canopy that no human artist has ever had the power to ornament.

Still more of the old idolatry of royalty you can see near this in the *Musée des Voitures,* where there is a collection of state carriages. These are great lumbering coaches, heavily bedecked with gold. The hubs and spokes of the wheels, the axles and parts of the body of the coach, are burdened with gold. They remind one of the circus wagon that excited so much interest on the village streets in our childhood.

" The King used this one on a certain occasion," "the Queen rode in that one," " the Pope was offered a seat in this one," " the royal baby was taken to the christening in that one," etc. I do not care to remember what they were all used for. I am not much of a royalist, and am sure that better men and women have taken far sweeter and brighter babies to be baptized in some country school-house, traveling in road-wagons or ox-carts.

But we come to the little palace—*Petit Trianon* — with greater interest. This palace Louis XVI. gave to Marie Antoinette. Here the King and Queen played rulers, and a sad and tragical play they made of it. The Empress Eugenie collected many of the belongings of Marie Antoinette and arranged them in the rooms of the *Petit Trianon,* where we saw them.

Her bed, and lamp, and jewe'-case, and work-stand, and pictures, reveal the exquisite taste of one over whose life aspersions were cast and sorrows rested. Let us draw over it the cloak of charity.

We pass out through the gates down to the little stream, where these rulers, who ought to have been caring for France, played miller and dairy-maid, while the people hungered for bread. By the spring-house wall is the statue of the shepherd, made by the Queen's order, standing there to-day as a monument to her folly.

A soldier accompanies us, for it is necessary to guard the treasures of the park, as well as the palace. He pointed out an old willow tree, saying that Marie Antoinette had planted it with her own hands. Several of our party took out their knives and began to hew it down for relics. I asked a lady, who spoke both French and English, for the word for " thieves." She told me, "*voleurs*," and I immediately shouted it to the soldier. He looked at me, and I pointed to the tree. The doctor was there. I would now have my revenge for all the reproofs he had given me. He would be arrested, and I would pay his fine to get him released, and then would make him promise obedience to me forever.

The soldier, smiling, went on. I shouted " *Voleures!*" but this time he did not even look back. I shouted

" *Voleurs !* " the third time; but he had no mercy, and
would not arrest the party.   The doctor came up and
offered me a chip, which I put away.   Then I told him
that Marie Antoinette had never planted the tree at all;
it was a trick of the soldiers who had to keep the park
in order, to get American travelers to clear away the
old trees for them, and that as soon as they had this
one cut up, he would show them another!   The doctor,
however, asserted that the soldier was so much amused
at an Irishman trying to talk French, that he could
not have collected himself to arrest them if they had
been carrying away the whole place.   Then I asked
him why it was that he and the other wood-carvers all
got behind the tree when I called.   The case was
getting desperate, and in my disappointment at not
having him arrested I was not willing to be trifled
with.   He answered that they had all been so much
ashamed of me they had gone behind the tree to hide
their blushes!   Then I felt sure that he was getting
jealous of my French accent.

But shall we turn to a dark page in history?   Re-
trace your steps to the palace at Versailles.   The
road will lead you along the borders of lakelets and
by great flower-beds, which are to-day as bright as they
were in 1789.   Enter once more the splendid structure.   It is not far in life between a smile and a tear;

between the mill and dairy and the guillotine, but a few months may intervene.

On October 5, 1789, a mob is formed in Paris, many of whom are women, driven mad by hunger and by liquor. This mob marches all the way from Paris to Versailles and surrounds the royal palace with cries of "bread!" and "vengeance!"

Here is the window where the beautiful Queen appears before the mob. She has ruled the people before by her queenly presence and beauty. She will appear again, and with a single wave of her hand calm the raging billows of popular wrath, even as the Savior calmed the waves of troubled Galilee. They are howling like maddened wolves about the window; but she has excited their applause; she has been their idol; she will be their idol still! Surely they have not forgotten her gracious acts; the pardon which she extended to an officer, with the words, "The Queen does not remember the quarrel, and the officer should not recollect what she has forgotten."

The people surely have not forgotten the taxes she has remitted, the hospitals she has builded for the poor, the cottages she has erected for the humble and lowly. But the people who form this mob have suffered much from misrule, and the long march from the city has not lessened their fury. The Queen goes to the window; but a raging, seething sea of hate boils before her, at the sight of which her face is blanched. The mob forces an entrance to the palace. A guard steps to the hallway, and shouting, "Save the Queen!" resists the progress of the people. He is slain in the doorway, and his blood crimsons the floor of the palace. Another guard takes his place and gives his life for the Queen. I saw the secret door and stairway by which she flees. At last the guards drive the mob from the palace. Some time the next day she again is forced to appear before the people, now only held back by the power of arms. The mob is sullen as before. Her power is gone, and she stands pale and trembling before the enraged and hungry throng. A man, whose name sends a thrill of devotion through every true American heart, uses his power to exorcise the demon of evil from the multitude before him. He stands by the Queen, whom they refuse to recognize. They would honor him, but they hate her. He takes her fair, white hand in his, and partly lifting it, and partly bowing to it, presses it to his lips.

A shout of joy arises! The demon of hate is gone! That one act of devotion to his Queen touches a chord in the fickle heart of the French that quickly responds to his desires.

La Fayette kisses the hand of Marie Antoinette.

The billows of wrath roll away, and the people shout praises in place of curses. But now a demand comes. The King and Queen of France must live in their palace, among the people in Paris. The procession is formed and the royal residence is taken up in the palace of the Tuilleries. The rest of that short, sad story is too well known. Let us reënter Paris and now visit the old city prison. It is not easy to gain admittance, but it is possible. I stand in the low, damp, narrow cell, where she who came to France when a child of sixteen, and who began her reign as the popular idol, was imprisoned. The same bars are on the little window; the same crucifix, before which she bowed, is on the wall; the same old-fashioned lamp, where the smoking flax gave forth a sickly flame, is above you. Here she sat knitting a garter for a friend.

She may have been a foolish queen, but she was a noble prisoner. Her shoes were soaked with water, and her dress was in tatters, but she uttered no complaint. If she had been a thoughtless queen, these chill walls, could they only speak, would tell a story of penitence that must have been heard by Him who said "Neither do I condemn thee; go and sin no more."

Out of the darkness there comes light. There is a God in history, because there is a God in providence. The Revolution was a necessity.

Let us look once more at the "Lion of Lucerne," carved in the rock, protecting the lily with his paw, while a broken spear transfixes his heart, and deem it not unmanly to drop a tear for the brave and also for the erring. The lion commemorates the bravery of the Swiss guard, every man of which fell defending the Tuilleries. Louis XVI. was tried and condemned for treason and was guillotined on January 25, 1793. On October 14th, Marie Antoinette was summoned before the tribunal at two o'clock in the morning. Her trial was one to bring the blush of shame to the most hardened cheeks. Justice was mocked, and civility, not to say decency, was outraged; yet she was calm and dignified, exhibiting in the highest degree the qualities of a true queen—a true woman. The day following her trial she was led to the guillotine. She arrayed herself in pure white linen, carefully arranged her hair, and with her arms bound behind her back was taken to the *Place de la Revolution*. Misfortune, detraction, and sorrow had subdued her nature and added to her better qualities a peculiar charm. It was easy for her to be calm when seated on the throne, but it was noble to be courteous and self-possessed when she ascended the scaffold. The knife descended, and she was with an impartial Judge, while the Revolution, in the language of Lamartine, was "irretrievably disgraced."

Paris has not disappointed me in the vastness of its buildings, the beauty of its boulevards, the displays of art, the wealth of its historical associations, nor in the generous policy of its government. I am told that a cool breeze or a shower of rain would have given freshness to that which seemed dull and without life. Yet as I recall the city I am forced to admit its beauty, notwithstanding its dust and drought. It is a city that has done much to preserve what is fairest in art, and the time may come when the same bell that rang out the order for massacre shall call together a people who will worship God in the sweet simplicity of an intelligent faith.

The French are a great people. They have displayed an energy in rising after defeat that astonishes the world. They are both watchful and courageous, warm in friendship, swift in battle, and terrible in resentment. The little children sit in the schools of patriotism and are taught to say, " *La belle France.*" In any possible conflict that may arise with the church or with a foreign foe, the French people would send up a mighty shout that would echo from the Pyrenees to the Straits, " *Vive la République !* " She is happy and contented as a republic, and will not return to a kingly form of government while enjoying her present prosperity. The old palaces and coin and monuments will be all the relics of royalty she desires, and these do not deplete her treasury. The site of the Tuilleries has become a garden for the people, and the children of poverty can play where monarchs sat enthroned.

CHAPTER XIII.

THERE is very little to interest one on the way from Paris to London, unless it is when crossing the straits. When we neared Calais, I thought of Beau Brummel, who was forced to flee from London to avoid the payment of his debts, and who, thus cast out of fashionable society, remarked that "Any man ought to be contented who could spend his time between Paris and London." Almost unconsciously, I put my hand to my neck-tie, to know that it was in proper position, and felt glad that this man had at least conferred one blessing on mankind, in doing away with the old padded ties that men used to bundle up their necks with. It seems rather strange that his name should have endured so long, since he was only an educated, polite, well-dressed spendthrift. But for many years he was the intimate associate of the royalty and nobility of London. This made the young man vain, and he presumed too much on his position, and on one occasion, when at dinner at the Carlton House, addressed the Prince of Wales in a very familiar manner:

" Wales, ring the bell ! "

The Prince obeyed, and when the footman appeared, said:

" Call Mr. Brummel's carriage."

Though Mr. Brummel denied this, it gained credence, and has passed into history. But when he had fallen into disfavor with the Prince, he was able to gain an advantage through the Prince's rudeness. Mr. Brummel, with three of his friends, gave a great *fête*, to which the Prince was invited. He accepted the invitation, and when passing the hosts, bowed most graciously to three of them, and passed Brummel without the slightest recognition. Mr. Brummel felt the insult keenly, but happened to know that the Prince was very sensitive on account of his corpulency ; so he violated the rules of ordinary hospitality by asking, loud enough for the Prince to hear him:

"Alvanley, who is your fat friend ? "

The Straits of Dover were on their good behavior, and the hour and a half on the water was very enjoyable after so many days of heat and dust. The chalk-white cliffs of England seemed to bid us welcome to a land which is nearer home than any other. Shakespeare's Cliff is more interesting than Tower Hill, though the latter is crowned with an old castle. We have seen so many old castles that we have lost interest in them.

What idiots most tourists are! They will spend time and money to get near or into some old castle, and after climbing up its narrow stone stairways, and rambling over its walls, will stop when they get ten miles away from it and obtain a field-glass to see what it looks like. They are excited about being able to see the ivy on the walls, and the very stones of the towers. It may be that some people are like old towers—they look better in the distance; but if they do, it is silly to try to bring them nearer to us by telescopes.

A young man said to me some years ago: "We have the queerest family you ever met; they are never happy when separated; they are continually trying to get together again; and as soon as they meet, they begin to quarrel." Tourists who have seen nothing interesting in the castles when visiting them, strain their eyes to look back when ten or twenty miles away. But it is one of the happy provisions of nature that the highest joy is sometimes afforded by the memory, which, like an accommodating sieve, has allowed all that was to be rejected to pass through, and retains that which has the elements of true pleasing.

We are in London—the pride of England and the wonder of the world. It is possible only to give impressions of the city as it appeared to me. It might look different to other eyes. Paris is gay, London is grave; Paris is smiling, London is thoughtful;

Paris is dressed in evening costume, London wears a business suit; Paris is going to the opera, London is on her way to the market; Paris is bent on pleasure, London thinks of business.

The houses are nearly uniform in size, seldom being more than six stories in height. The architecture is simple and solid, almost severe. The houses where wealth abounds do not have an attractive external appearance.

Some of the more prominent business streets are so crowded with omnibuses and wagons that it is slow traveling through them, and requires some skill to cross them. The drivers are experts, and carriages dash by each other so closely that the stranger holds his breath and braces up his nerves for collisions.

The best way to see the city is from the top of an omnibus, which accommodates about twenty persons, and where lap-robes are in readiness in case of rain. It has not the hurry of Chicago, and can afford to stop while the passenger climbs down from the top. The streets are smooth and clean, being constantly swept by boys, who, with pan and broom, dart in among the teams at the risk of their lives, depositing their collections in iron boxes by the curb. These boxes are emptied by night, the contents being valuable for the farm and garden.

All teams keep to the left, in place of to the right,

13

as with us. This seriously endangers the pedestrian who has been accustomed to look for danger in an opposite direction. But it is true of many tourists and others that they look the wrong way for trouble.

The English people are very polite; not so demonstratively so as the French, but substantially so. The Frenchman will ask you to accept some hospitality that he knows it is impossible for you to receive, and appear surprised and grieved that you decline it. When he knows that you may have another engagement at the same hour, he will express his deep regret, and urge you all the more to do him the exceeding honor that he solicits. If the Englishman knows that you can not comply with the request, he will keep his invitation in his pocket, and tell you that he intended to invite you, but that he had heard with regret of your having a previous engagement. He is substantially polite. I have formed an exalted opinion of our English cousins, and am in a mood to honor the memory of my great grandfather, who kept hounds and horses in old England. The reader will excuse me for referring to him, inasmuch as he never killed anyone, or otherwise rose to prominence, but somehow it is irreverent to neglect the old, in the Old World.

I have wondered how everybody knows that we are foreigners, and Americans. What is there peculiar about us, to enable the citizens of other countries to say at once "Americans"? A lady told us, it was by our noses. The doctor felt flattered, for his nasal member is well proportioned and shapely, but I immediately proceeded to humble him, by assuring him that they always took me for an American, and if it was by our noses, then my nose must be an exact counterpart of his own. The logic could not be improved. If things that are equal to the same thing are equal to each other, things that look like the same thing must resemble each other.

There may be something about the dress, or manner, that enables the world to tell us where we belong. There is a "shibboleth" that betrays us. A young graduate of Oxford talked with me about it. He claimed that he could distinguish me by Western slang. I allowed my pride to resent this, and when he asked me how I knew where he belonged, I told him of the cockney speech. We then agreed to talk rationally, and whenever I would use a Western term he was to rap on the table; and whenever he would use a peculiarly English word, or phrase, I would rap. In a little while I forgot all about the contract, as we had been earnestly discussing the problem of municipal government. He brought down his knuckles on the table with so much vigor that he startled me. I had used a word that is as familiar in Chicago as the name of the city. He had never heard it, and did not know what it meant. I looked at him with a feeling of surprise. He must have lived on some "Island of the Blessed," never to have heard the word "boodle." Then I engaged him more closely, and introduced the McKinley bill. If you want to make an Englishman utterly oblivious to everything on earth, and in heaven, except the theme you introduce, just talk of the McKinley bill. He replied with an eagerness that was beyond control:

"Don't you know, my dear fellow—"

Down came my knuckles on the table, with more vigor than he had used; but it took me some minutes to get him far enough from the McKinley bill to recall the fact that we had an arrangement to call time, when any anglicism was used. Then he said he was very much mortified that he had been so grossly familiar, but the American tariff always made him forget the proprieties of life.

But while we discover each other's nationality, the people go wildly astray over our business, or professions. I have more of a medical than ministerial look, and the doctor's gentleness and black clothes give him a sort of sanctimonious appearance. The reader will kindly take another look at his portrait and verify my words. But if he were to go out with a manuscript sermon, and I with a case of surgical instruments, or with prescription blanks, the world might be just as sinful, and somewhat more ailing than it was before. " It is better, therefore, for us to suffer the ills we have, than to flee to others that we know not of."

Saint Paul's is one of the central points of London. The building itself is an imposing one, and the services conducted within its walls are about as cold as the crypt beneath it. A few days after having attended religious worship there, I returned to visit the crypt. It is a cold, damp, dreary basement, more like a dungeon than a church, and is also extensively used as a burial place for the illustrious. I can not appreciate the good taste of anyone who would want to have his friends buried under the slab pavement of Saint Paul's. It is cold and chilly, and in every sense gloomy. I can go to the graves of the poor, out on the hill-side, where the ivies creep above the remains, and the buttercups come up in spring-time, and the robins swing their mates on the blackberry briars, and the red clover breathes its sweet perfume, and the sun bathes the little hillock, and the morning dews sparkle with the brightness of diamonds, and the gentle showers fall, and the white-sheeted snow piles up its castles, and the ice forms its crystals; but what possible pleasure a friend could have in going down into this sub-cellar, and stalking along by artificial light, and reading on the dull slab that covers the body, the name that once was so dear to him, I can not possibly conjecture. I never saw the beauty of those words till now: "Blessed are the dead that the rain rains on." Visit the crypt at Saint Paul's, and you will be very dull indeed if you fail to see the blessedness of having a sepulcher out of doors.

Christopher Wren, whose genius as an architect would have been even more apparent had he not been hindered in his plans by the stupid interference of James II., is buried here. It is said that he wept when he saw his fair plans so cruelly marred. After a blameless and honored life he died at an advanced age. A black marble slab marks his resting place, on which is an inscription in Latin :

"If you seek his monument, look about you."

But, as I have noted, that monument would have been more worthy, had it not been marred by one who had blind devotion, but no conception of true art. But it is not in Saint Paul's alone that the genius of Wren was displayed. In nearly every art of London his plans were copied, and many structures were reared under his direction. The great fire gave him an opportunity for the fullest exhibition of his talents.

In this same dull crypt are the sarcophagi of Nelson and Wellington, whose names are interwoven with the history of England, and whose military genius changed the world's map. In a separate apartment is the car used at Wellington's funeral. It is made from cannon captured from the French. It weighs eighteen tons, and is without any particular attraction, except its bigness and the use to which it was put.

The efforts made to honor Nelson and Wellington have signally failed, because the memorials erected are not at all equal to the greatness of the patriots in whose honor they stand, and because the memorials themselves are not well chosen. The prosperity and liberty of a nation are better memorials than marble and bronze. The time has come when institutions of charity or education, founded in the name of patriots, will be considered more attractive than the lumbering funeral car, or tall shaft. The Wellington school or the Nelson hospital would outlive the monument.

I left the crypt of Saint Paul's, wondering why people will go down there to worship. I can see some fitness in a demoniac living among the tombs, but no fitness in making the church a sepulcher.

As I was leaving the church I stopped for a few minutes to look at the Gordon memorial slab placed in one of the aisles. The inscription would appear bombastic were it not prompted by a brother's love. Its statements are exaggerated and ought to have been reviewed before allowing them to find a place in the temple of the True. The inscription is :

"Major-General Charles George Gordon, who at all times and everywhere gave his strength to the weak, his substance to the poor, his sympathy to the suffering, and his heart to God. He saved an empire by his warlike genius. He ruled vast provinces with justice, wisdom, and power; and lastly, obedient to his sovereign's command, he died in the heroic attempt to save men, women, and children from imminent and deadly peril."

Part of this inscription appears like irony. There is a general conviction in the minds of all who revere the name of Gordon that his sovereign ought to have supported, as well as commanded, so worthy a subject, and that with proper support, he, and those for whom he died, might have been saved from peril.

The criticism on the British government in this respect seems just, and yet no one believes that Gordon was willfully abandoned. At most it was an error in judgment, to which his own injudicious confidence largely contributed. The Lord did not work a miracle to deliver him, and he had no right to expect it. He should have first considered whether he were able to meet the enemy with the force at his command; and if not, he should have refused to imperil his own life. His generous impulses and his wonderful courage and philanthropy did not save him from the natural consequences of the battle he fought. His death was a loss to England, and being a loss to England is a loss to the world.

Nearly all Americans go to church in London. The arguments are manifold: They have nothing else to do; they want to hear the music; they want to see the building. At Saint Paul's, we heard the music and nothing else; at Westminster Abbey, we listened to a sermon by Archdeacon Farrar, that was of special merit. He began by a reference to the elections that are always in order throughout Britain, gave a picture of the sorrows of earth, referred to the Homestead riots in America, and finally pointed his hearers to Jesus, the hope of the nations. I would have enjoyed the sermon, had it not been for a sort of creepy sensation that comes over one when he is in a morgue! The Abbey was so full of dead kings and queens, and poets, and actors; it had in it so many effigies and wax figures, and marble statues, and monuments, that I could think of little else than "Meditations Among the Tombs." I had told the doctor that it would be wicked to look at the Abbey on the Sabbath; but when I saw it, and remembered how the good people used to go out during "intermission" and read the epitaphs on the tombstones in the church-yard, I was not sure but that I was getting too strict, or else the fathers and mothers ought not to have set us the example.

There was very little in the Abbey worthy of note.

as we learned on a subsequent visit, but epitaphs, and all the people buried in it were good. The tombstones lie about the bodies that lie under the tombstones! They would tell more lies about the dead if carving in stone were not so expensive.

I once called to see a lady, and her servant said to me that her mistress was not in; just then a member of the family appeared and informed me that *mater familias* was lying down up-stairs. " What an afflicted family ! " I muttered; "the mistress is lying down up-stairs and the servant is lying down-stairs! There will certainly be a death here soon."

But really there are many great people buried here. There are monuments to some who have found tombs elsewhere; but if one sees the cenotaph, it matters little where the dust may be. There are kings, and queens, and lords, and earls, and dukes, and poets, and statesmen, and admirals, and generals, and painters, and discoverers, and scholars, and musicians, and actors, and singers, and princes, almost at will, buried in Westminster Abbey. It is a rich place to go if one cares to walk over royal dust, but really I prefer a house of worship that has more life in it. I suppose that it does not make much difference where we are buried, but I would prefer to be put away somewhere outside the church, where the little children may come to play on the grass, and try to spell out my name, the only words graven on the plain stone.

Doctor Parker preaches in the City Temple, a building that will accommodate a large congregation. It was late when we arrived, but a gentleman provided us with sittings. The singing was loud and measured. Its welling chorus reminded me of billows dashing against the shore. The voice of praise completely drowned the great organ. Then, in the solemn stillness, the minister began a sermon of telling power. It was one of those searching sort of discourses that makes a man look inside himself, to discover just how many mean things he has said, and done, and gives him a determination to be more charitable in judging his brother. But it must have been easy for Doctor Parker to preach, after such a song-service, and then I did not see any tombstones about. I think the appropriate hymn for Westminster would be, " Hark ! from the Tombs ! "

Though I have no appointment to make amendments in the hymnology of the Church of England, I think I could fix up a verse that would be appropriate when the Queen comes to service. It is not all original, and for that reason may not be adopted:

> Hark ! from the tombs the doleful sound !
>   Mine ears attend the cry,
> Lo ! England's Queen comes to the church
>   Where she must shortly lie.

The church where Mr. Spurgeon preached will always be called Spurgeon's church, no matter who the pastor may be. Everything about this church is plain. The windows are of plain glass. The seats are the most uncomfortable that ever mortal occupied, built with special adaptation to backache, and other forms of penance. I obtained a sitting on the shelf end of a pew that was about as large as a pie-pan, and inclined from the pew end, to which it was attached in such a way that I felt all the time as though I were sliding off. It was a good place to be impressed with the insecurity of all earthly possessions, and of the little that there is in them to give rest. The floor had not a shred of carpet on it, and looked as though it was a stranger to brooms and dust-pans. Galleries extend about the entire building, giving a very large seating capacity. The pulpit platform is very high, and reaches out in an oval shape quite a distance. The building was filled with a plain-looking people, many of whom were Americans, clad in their traveling clothes.

I was interested in the singing. So many people have praised the singing in Spurgeon's church that I anticipated something wonderful. The minister, in announcing the second hymn, told the congregation that it would not fit the tune to which it would be sung, and therefore he would adjust the last line of each verse to it, There seemed to be no good way of stretching out the tune ; so he proceeded to amend the hymn by cutting off several syllables from the last line of each verse. Old Pocustes never haggled so wretchedly at the legs of his victims as did the preacher with the last lines. He read every verse, doctoring the elongated part of it as he went along. The people sang with a loud noise, but without any skill. They had no organ to regulate them, and hold back the too willing ones, and pull up the laggards. But they had also forgotten and differently interpreted the corrections made on the verses, and when they came to these places it was like a team of horses. attempting to pull a heavy load, by starting one at a time; or, like a wagon going over the corduroy roads we made through Southern swamps in war times. They jerked, and jarred, and hesitated, and started up. One thought he knew it better than the others, and increased his vocal utterance to a shriek. The rest came in sure but slow. When all were done singing, near me, an echo came down from the upper galleries, or what seemed to be an echo. It was the lingering notes of musical stragglers, who were a few seconds too late getting into camp.

I have always admired Mr. Spurgeon's sermons. His name towers aloft above the ministers of his age, like some tall oak above the trees of the forest ; but I recognized his greatness more after attending a service in the church he left, than ever I did before. People who came to such a house, and engaged in such services, must have been attracted by the majestic power of the minister of the Gospel. Let not those who have not been endowed as he attempt to do what he did. Without a change in the house, and conduct of worship, the successor must fail, and his failure will be attributed to him, when he might have succeeded if rightly seconded by some regard to that which is comely and engaging, in the worship of Him whose glory filled the temple.

The Parliament Houses were originally the royal palace. The buildings that formerly stood here were destroyed by fire, and the present immense structure, covering eight acres, has risen since 1840. It is situated on the Thames, and parts of the building are below the river at high tide. Such stupidity in architecture can not easily be forgiven. The buildings cost about fifteen million dollars. Visitors are hurried through the palace, and but little opportunity afforded for seeing the different rooms. The rooms that interest us most are those occupied by the two Houses of Parliament. The royal robing rooms are not worth seeing, unless one has enough weakness in his nature to regard with reverence the place where the waiting ladies unhook the royal robes and fasten up the royal bonnet-strings.

But we do take a deep interest in the halls where England's wit and wisdom have for years been displayed, and where English law has been framed, and where patriots have had the courage to plead for the rights of humanity. The windows in the Prince's chamber display the rose, and thistle, and shamrock. The throne, under a gilded canopy, is at one end of the room occupied by the Lords. In front of the throne, and elevated a little from the floor, is the famous wool-sack of the Lord Chancellor. It is simply a sack of wool about four feet square, and covered with red cloth. This he occupies when presiding over the Lords. It is emblematic of the fact that wool used to be considered the staple product of Great Britain. This great red ottoman has neither arms nor back to it; and unless his lordship is supported by the dignity of his office, he must have rather an uncomfortable time of it.

The clock-tower on the north of the palace is three hundred and eighteen feet high. The clock has four faces, and each dial is twenty-three feet in diameter. It takes just five hours to wind up the striking portion of the clock. The bell is a marvel in size, weighing thirteen tons, and can be heard over the city. It is familiarly called "Big Ben," after the commissioner of works at the time it was placed in the tower. To the dismay of the architects, the bell was found to have a flaw in it, which soon developed into a crack. To take it down and recast it involved great labor and expense. A skillful man suggested that, possibly, if the crack were filed open, it might remove the jarring noise. The little crack was offensive; but when the filers had made a wide opening, old Ben's voice was as distinct, and clear, and silvery, as ever it had been.

The Parliament Houses are most carefully guarded. Ladies carrying satchels or little parcels are compelled to leave them in a waiting-room. Dynamite is the dread of royalty, and even a little hand-satchel might contain it.

One day a proposal was made that we go to Greenwich observatory. I eagerly accepted the offer, and found several pleasant companions on the way. Just what we went for I could not tell. I knew, but rather disliked to admit, the truth. There is a ball on the observatory that slowly rises a few minutes before one o'clock each afternoon, and descends precisely at one, communicating with wires throughout the kingdom of Great Britain and giving the time. Cannon are fired by the current as far north as Edinburgh Castle.

We wanted to see the ball go up and come down.

As we waited at the boat landing, someone proposed to get weighed, and I, finding that a stranger was willing to drop the penny in the slot, mounted the scales. The hands turned to the proper place. I wiped my glasses, to get the exact weight, when, to my surprise, I discovered that I weighed fourteen and three-fourths stone. I squandered a penny of my own on a fellow who stood by, and asked him quietly how many pounds made a stone. He said, in a low tone of voice, "Fourteen pounds!" None of the rest were willing to be weighed, until I, ashamed of their ignorance, told them I would calculate their weight for them if they would not permit these Englishmen to know how little they knew.

We rode under the London Bridge and all the other bridges between London and Greenwich, climbed the high hill to the observatory, and sat down on some iron benches to see the ball go up. We waited until three minutes past one, and the ball did not rise. Then a man came out and said that the ball never rose when the wind was blowing, but that he would like to have pay for the seats we had occupied. It happened that the ladies of the party were all sitting at the time. One of the gentlemen protested against charging for seats in a public park, but they had to pay for them. I wanted him to prove that I had been seated. He could not get anyone to witness against me, and said he had not seen me on a chair and could not charge me. I told him I would not witness in the case, inasmuch as if I did, the ladies would certainly have to

14

pay for my chair too, and that would not be honorable in me; besides we had come four thousand miles, and he did not have the show come off according to agreement. It might also be better for him to be on his guard, for when Americans paid for chairs in a public park they were liable to take them home with them.

There was little else of interest at Greenwich, and we did not propose to spend another day waiting to see a little ball run up and down a ten-foot pole; so we returned to the city. On the way a boat took fire a short distance from us, and we watched the brave fellows steering it to the shore, at the risk of their lives. Two men on our boat lost their hats. The first man was too drunk to appreciate his loss, but the other one called lustily to some men in a skiff to save his beaver. It was finally restored to him for a six-pence. It was a genuine silk hat, and when he wiped it and put it on his head it looked as shiny and sleek as a seal that has just climbed out of the water. I never saw a hat come from the iron more glossy. If anyone wants to experiment with his own hat by dipping it in water, I shall not make any charge for the suggestion, but he will please not hold me responsible for the result. I saw but one experiment, and it might not always result as this one did.

If you have any regard for your good name, never take a boat-ride on the Thames. Come to Chicago and enjoy a pleasure trip on our river, but do not waste time and money seeking pleasure on the Thames! The excursionists are generally of the lowest class. One gentleman warned me of the danger of losing my watch. I thanked him, and was careful when he came near me.

CHAPTER XIV.

WE went by the underground road to the Tower. The road is not entirely successful. The air is not pure, and the fumes emitted by the engine are both unpleasant and dangerous. No city ought to permit such a method of travel, unless some motive power is used that will leave the tunnel free from smoke and sulphur. The Tower is a fortress, and has been variously used as a palace, and prison, and museum. It was evidently intended at first to be a defense against a foreign foe, and then to be a terror to the foe at home. It was built so as to withstand an attack from without and within the city. The Tower stands near the Thames, and prisoners of state were usually brought inside the Tower through the Traitors' Gate by a sort of sluice communicating with the river.

Many old pieces of artillery, which were captured by the British troops, or presented to the government by conquered or friendly powers, are parked inside the walls. If anyone has never seen the ancient armor, he will be repaid for an investigation of the panoply of the olden time. But that which interests most visitors is the collection of crown jewels, securely guarded, but well displayed: The crowns worn by the sovereigns of England; the diamonds on their armor; the precious jeweled garter, with the memorable words, " *Honi soit qui mal y pense,*" embroidered in gold beneath it. If the story of the latter be true, that Edward III. courteously handed the garter of the Countess of Salisbury to her, and when several Lords smiled at him, replied, "Evil to him who evil thinks," his vow has been fulfilled, for it has become the most honored order in Europe, and the men think themselves happy who are privileged to wear it. Royal scepters, and rods of equity, and baptismal fonts, and bracelets, are shown, to the delight of the visitor. These, to me, seem but the playthings of royalty; yet in a room near by you may see the axe of the executioner, iron thumb-screws and collars, and pincers whose heated fangs were fastened in the quivering flesh of the unfortunate. In one of these towers the most illustrious prisoners were confined : Wallace, Anne Boleyn, Lady Jane Grey, Cranmer, and Walpole. To this tower the seven bishops were brought by guards, who earnestly asked a blessing from the prisoners. Along these waters, and into this tower, by this detested gateway, these illustrious prisoners for principle were taken, while men saluted the barge and cried out, "God bless your lordships!" On these waters the cannon thundered forth the delight of the people when the bishops were released. In an adjoining tower the infamous Guy Fawkes, who, with others, conspired to destroy the King and the whole Parliament, was examined by torture. The Tower incloses about twelve acres, but in history it is the richest mine that has ever been created.

It is not my purpose to enter this department of investigation, but anyone who is at all familiar with prominent points in English history will recognize the Tower of London as the greatest historical center in all Europe. It combines all that is interesting in a palace with all that is gloomy in a prison ; all that is strong in a fortress with all that is educational in a museum. All that is terrible in tragedy, cruel in oppression, and noble in the courage of men and women, has been displayed within these narrow walls. Macaulay says that there is no sadder spot on earth than the little cemetery adjoining the Tower; but certainly the spot where the dust lies is not so sad as the place where torture and cruelty reigned, and where the blade of a terrible justice was made bare. In the memory of this, I left the Tower, and the historic events were to my mind more vivid, and the sufferers and sinners were more real, than the crowns and scepters and precious stones.

Why England should display a model of the Kohinoor, I can hardly guess. It was obtained by conquest; secured because she was stronger than the Rajah Singh's province. It takes away much of the brightness of the original treasure, and obscures all the light that might otherwise be reflected from the model. Neither a nation nor an individual should display jewels that have not been secured in an honorable way. A cannon whose use is destruction, or a flag that is carried as an incentive to battle, or a bugle that calls to arms, may be a rightful trophy; but that can not be so regarded whose highest purpose is to please. The Kohinoor in the crown of an Indian prince would be admired, but the same stone in England's jewel-case loses its beauty.

The National Gallery, in London, is made up of a very large collection of paintings, many of which are of merit. The names of two artists, however, were prominent in my desire to visit the gallery. Ruskin's wonderful word painting made me eager to see the works of his favorite, Turner. I confess to a feeling of bitter disappointment in seeing Turner's paintings. He fails in color, proportion, and perspective. There is, incomparably, more beauty in Ruskin's word painting than can be found in Turner's brush work. The

author of " The Stones of Venice " pleads earnestly
for truth in art.   But dullness in art belies nature.
The fading leaf may have in it the distinct light of a
hundred flames and the blushing beauty of all the
fruits of the orchard.

But no one need be disappointed in Landseer.
Expect something wonderful, and you will find that
which exceeds your expectations.   His dogs and lions,
and other tame and wild animals, are wonderfully
true.   The eye has in it the sparkle of life, and this
living eye follows you with distinct plays of passion
and intelligence.   One can not look at the dogs without feeling, instinctively, that the dogs are watching
him.   He has studied position so well, that the idea
of constraint is lost.   It is difficult to express the
thought I have just now in mind ; but if the reader
has ever had a photograph taken in the old way,
where he had to sit bolt upright, with his head
fastened in an iron clamp, and remain thus for three
or four minutes, while the plate, falsely called " sensitive," was wrought on by the light, he will have the
idea I have of constraint in position.

In his " Dignity and Impudence " the great, good-
natured dog remains serene and unruffled in the presence of the little upstart cur.   Who has not seen men
posing before the world in the same relative attitude
as Landseer's dogs?   One hardly knows which is the

more striking — the self-possession of the mastiff or the self-importance of the cur that tries to stretch himself so far beyond himself. In the two dozen rooms are thirteen hundred pictures, some of which have been in the palaces of kings, and others that have been purchased at fabulous prices.

If one were to visit London and see nothing but the British Museum, he would be amply repaid. This was begun as a library in 1753, valued then at two hundred and fifty thousand dollars. It has grown from that time in almost everything that will interest the student, no matter in what department of science he may desire to extend his investigations. The genius of Pericles and the skill of Phidias are to be seen in the marbles brought from Athens. The cradle of the race — Egypt — has been despoiled to contribute to this wonderful museum. Many students go to London and remain in the museum day after day for months, and even for years, and then come away unsatisfied with the little they have learned of all that is to be discovered there. Thousands of articles have been collected in the different galleries that date back many centuries before the coming of Christ. The attempt, therefore, to give the names of objects of interest would be useless.

The Rosetta stone is not of secondary importance to the student. This is a tablet of black rock that is the key to the interpretation of the hieroglyphics of Egypt. This language was never translated until some time after the discovery of this stone. It was found by the French near the Rosetta mouth of the Nile, about the year 1799, but came into the possession of the English in 1802. There is an inscription on this stone in three languages : The first was the sacred hieroglyphics ; the second the common Egyptian; and the third the Greek. It was suggested that the inscription might be the same in each language, and by a comparison of the second and third they were found to be so. It was then believed that the first, or hieroglyphic language, recorded the same thing contained in the second and third languages. If so, there was a key to the first, and by patient study an interpretation was given it which corresponded with that of the other two. Then the hieroglyphics on the Rosetta stone, as interpreted, were applied to other inscriptions on monuments and tombs and coffins in which mummies were laid away. The Rosetta stone thus became a rude dictionary of the oldest language, hieroglyphics, and by this means the most important discoveries have been made, and truths of history, especially of sacred history, have been verified.

One can not but wonder at the singular providence by which such vast treasures have thus been opened up in the field of archæological research. Copies of the inscription have been multiplied, and there is no danger of the knowledge being lost.

The medal and ornament room is closed; but by ringing a bell, and submitting to a little inspection, you may be admitted, after registering your name. The treasures of this room are rich and rare. They consist of ornaments, and coins of gold, and are of very ancient periods.

In this room is the elegant and far-famed Portland vase, found in a tomb near Rome, in the early part of the seventeenth century. It is of blue glass, with different designs in white. Although but small in comparison with many richly-ornamented vases, it is very highly prized. In 1845 a man subject to temporary fits of insanity was looking at it. A loose brick was in the pavement, which the maniac picked up, and in an instant broke the vase into small fragments. A photograph of the little pieces hangs on the wall, and one hardly knows whether to admire more the vase itself, or the skill displayed in putting the pieces together again. It is only by close inspection that you can see the seams where it has been united.

One day we turned away from city sight-seeing to visit the Queen's palace at Windsor, twenty-seven miles from London. The palace is delightfully situated near the Thames, and from the Tower an extended view is afforded. The rooms of the palace were, however, so far inferior to those we had seen elsewhere, that we were willing to vary our experience by taking a look at the stables. One hundred horses are kept up in splendid style in these stables, for the use of the royal family. Costly harness and saddles for these are shown. Every riding horse has its own bridle and saddle, though some of the bits have not been in the horse's mouth for years, and the saddle may never have been on his back. It is doubtful whether Her Majesty has ever seen half the horses kept here for her use, and the one which she rode many years ago is pointed to with a sort of satisfaction by the attendant, as though it were worthy of a little veneration. The Lord of the Queen's stables is an important personage, and remembers well what horse has been most highly honored.

Many of the Queen's subjects never sat in a carriage or rode an hour on horseback. Many of her subjects, shut in by wasting diseases, would have been greatly benefited by a little outing in one of the coaches that has not been used for several years. The use, too, would have been good for the horses, that would be all the better for a little exercise. The attendant showed us the carriage in which General Grant rode, when the Queen entertained him, on his visit to Windsor. It certainly is not necessary to keep up a coach just because the honored American used it.

The more I see of castles and palaces, and now, stables, and the forced inequalities of life, the more heartily do I thank God that I am an American citizen and am not taxed to support royal pensioners. American poverty is not forced to contribute to supply the table of a family that has no claim on it, and but little sympathy with it.

On our way back we stopped at Slough, which was the home of Herschel, the great astronomer, and engaged a carriage for a drive to Stoke Poges and Burnham Beeches. The church-yard at Stoke Poges is the scene of Gray's Elegy, whose sad, sweet lines have gone through all the world. We took a branch of the old yew tree under which the poet penned these lines:

> The boast of heraldry, the pomp of power,
>   And all that beauty, all that wealth e'er gave
> Await alike the inevitable hour —
>   The path of glory leads but to the grave.

Did he write the poem when seated beneath the tree? Probably not; the poem indicates that he did not, but you get all the benefits of association and give value to the twig cut off, by exercising a little credulity.

The epitaph to his mother, by whose side he is buried, is very touching, because of what is delicately hinted at, rather than boldly expressed. It concludes:

"Here sleep the remains of Dorothy Gray, widow; the careful, tender mother of many children, one of whom alone had the misfortune to survive her."

Near by is the farm of William Penn, in one of the fields of which is a tall cenotaph to Gray, erected by the Penn heirs, with some verses of the elegy engraven on it. An old lady at the gate sells copies of the elegy at a penny each. The whole scene about Stoke Poges is one of peace and rest. There was nothing pretentious in the grave-yard; nothing of the rivalry that cemeteries display in rearing taller shafts to the departed, thus keeping up class divisions, even among the tombs.

In the fields adjoining, a herd of deer were quietly resting, without fear and undisturbed. A few miles further on we come to the Burnham Beeches, which are famed as the finest in England. The trees are very old, and show their age in their size and ruggedness. They have grown to measure many feet in circumference and have the usual gnarled and broken appearance of the same variety of trees in America.

The next evening we went by train to the Crystal Palace. This immense structure is built after the manner of a conservatory of flowers. Allow your imagination to have a green-house several stories high. Inside, there are flowers in the different galleries, and as much cheap stuff offered for sale as you will find in any shopping place, together with eating apartments, saloons, and theaters, cheap pictures and poor sculpture. Fifty thousand people had come out to witness the display of fireworks. They saw the rockets go up and heard an occasional thud as the sticks came down.

They clapped their hands when the set pieces were fired. Then it grew dark and I heard someone say :

"The same old show! Let us get to the train." A scramble and race to the various stations followed, and those who secured seats were considered very fortunate.

The doctor drew the line at the Zoological Gardens. I could not persuade him to go with me. He evidently must have had a surfeit of circuses and animal shows when he was a boy. But I may as well confess, that I have a passion for animal shows, and can sit or stand for an hour watching the bears scramble for position in the park dens of our city.

There is much to be learned from the habits of the black bear. He is so human in many of his ways. One day, when about to leave Lincoln Park, in Chicago, I heard a great commotion in the pit where a half dozen black bears are kept. There was evidently a bear fight. I have often gone to meetings to hear men disputing ; why not go and take a lesson from the bears about the proper method of conducting an argument. In the center of the pit a dead tree had been placed for the use of the animals. It was strong enough to support all the bears in the pit, if each of them could agree as to the limb he would rest on. A black bear that would weigh three hundred pounds had gone up on the tree, and gracefully adjusting his head on one limb and his body on two, was soon fast asleep. The children had been looking on with wonder, and probably some words of praise had been uttered by the fair sex. A king was once jealous of his future son-in-law for a somewhat similar reason, and why should not the bears be jealous because of ill-advised praise? An envious brother bear that weighed a little more than the bear in the tree stood on the stones below and bore it as long as he could. Then his spirits rose to the occasion and he began to growl.

Men sometimes growl, as well as bears!

Bruin below looked up enviously at bruin above.

"What is that little upstart doing there? Come down."

Bruin above seemed to real ize a principle of law, common among men, that possession is nine points in his favor. Bruin below intimated his rights by another growl, which I easily interpreted to mean:

"Might gives right."

Such things have been heard among men. The audience was divided in its sympathy, not an uncommon thing either, but was not sufficiently interested to interfere. The big brother grew impatient and started up the tree. They growled, and snarled, and struck out with their paws. The argument was against the smaller bear. It is that way with men. The position was not good for a free fight, but the elevation made it all the more attractive. It is that way among human contestants. The little bear went down the tree with more of haste than gracefulness, and was snarled at by his brother. He slunk away to his den, and did not look out again, reminding me much of half of the politicians the morning after an election. "To the victors belong the spoils," and so this victor took the fat place vacated by the smaller bear. He had about him an air of self-possession, as he was in fact in the absolute enjoyment of tree possession.

He licked his paws, looked out contentedly at the audience, and then, to show his indifference to the popular feeling, stretched himself out and closed his eyes, and slept like the historical babe in the nursery rhyme, on the tree top. I came home, and read in one of the evening papers about two French gentlemen who settled their quarrel, on the field of honor, with knives and pistols! What a splendid thing it is to be a man! How glad we ought to be that we are not black bears! ✓

I always learn something at the Zoo, and the visit to the London Garden, with its multitude of birds and

15

beasts, was not an exception. A substantial structure contains dens of lions, leopards, and tigers. It was near the time for feeding the animals, and how impatient they became! They walked about as impatiently as some men do when dinner is but a few minutes late. The roaring of the lions was something terrible as they waited for their food. At last it was thrown to them in great pieces. I saw them eating, crushing bones, and tearing the flesh with their teeth. I watched them licking their greasy paws, and when they had used their tongues as napkins they stretched themselves out to sleep.

"If thine enemy hunger, feed him."

Among lions and men I discovered that a good meal is a great aid in peace-making. There are some creatures, called husbands, who are as impatient as tigers, until they are fed, and then they lie down and sleep without any expression of gratitude, either to God or their wives; but the old advice holds good: "It is better to feed the beast!"

Returning to the city, I found the hotel crowded with Germans, fleeing from the cholera. Everybody was talking of it.

"It is in Paris;" "in London;" "in Liverpool;" "in Glasgow."

"It is on nearly every vessel!"

" My new dresses, that I bought in Paris, will be ruined ! "

"Aw! I preesoom that we will be fumigated, and never get the perfoom of the sulphur from our garments again. Aw ! "

" Doctor, do you really think there is any danger of our being kept in quarantine ? "

" The President of the United States will not allow any vessel to land unless kept in quarantine for twenty days ! "

Many talk as though they had no friends in America who might be exposed to the pestilence if strict laws were not made and enforced. The steamers are crowded, and large prices are offered for early ones, by people, who, a month ago, were clamoring for the privilege of staying abroad two weeks longer. It was refreshing to meet many, and among them delicate ladies, who had such sweet faith that they rested in perfect peace.

The doctor had taken so much interest in hospital work that I agreed to go to Scotland alone, and join him in Ireland in two weeks. I therefore hastily packed my trunk, took the doctor's hand, gave him some fatherly advice, and was off for the land of the thistle.

CHAPTER XV.

ON the way to Edinburgh we see the vast uncultivated estates that have been entailed and are kept up to gratify the tastes of some titled noblemen in hunting and grouse shooting. Telegraph wires were decorated with little pieces of white boards, to keep the birds from resting there. Their lives were to be saved from the dangers of electricity, to fall by the use of powder and lead.

The difference between these estates and the wide farms of the western parts of our country is marked. All our lands are subject to equal taxation. The game wardens are employed in keeping people from killing any sort of game on these pauper lands.

I suggested that the government could not hire men in America to attend to this sort of business. The fellow who would attempt it would discover that the lands were not well situated for health resorts.

We soon entered on a discussion of the causes and cures of poverty. It was animated, to say the least. There were ten persons in the compartment, of whom

I counted but one, and all the others were against me.
I modestly suggested that rum was a factor. The nine
all had liquor of some sort with them, and frequently
relieved their thirst by a glass of wine, beer, or whisky.
An old lady was traveling with her son, and she was
well provided with beer. I gave them a temperance
lecture, and suggested something about the influence
of a mother. She held the bottle in her hands a good
while, and then her appetite got the better of her and
she took a drink, and threw the half-emptied bottle
from the window of the compartment.

Then I suggested that the keeping up of a non-pro-
ducing aristocracy, whose luxuries were paid for by
the people, was a cause of poverty. I found here a
divided sentiment, when I modestly assured them that
an ex-President of the United States raised poultry,
and another practiced law, and inquired what profes-
sion the Prince of Wales had, or how he earned the
right to live? That was next door to high treason.
But I even suggested that the only things we knew of
that he certainly did, were play baccarat, and attend
horse races and prize fights.

The parties agreed that all they expected to make
was "a living." One of the ladies in the compartment was a farmer's wife, who had saved enough
money to make a visit to her mother. She told us
that she was prohibited from killing the hares that

destroyed the young trees in her garden. She was an intelligent lady, and her conversation showed both modesty and refinement. When I told them of forests where wood was free, and of tenants who were allowed all the timber they chose to use, and all the coal they cared to burn, and of the broad acres where absolute possession might be obtained, and of property subject to taxation, and of government officers paid but modest salaries, and retiring to private life to earn their own bread by their toil, and of the poorest of the people having wheat bread and golden butter, and meat, every day, all of whose houses had wooden floors, and of the wages they received for their toil, they looked at me with wonder, and said that they had heard of these things, but never believed them. I did not agree with them in anything, and yet, when we left the car, they all bade me good-by most heartily, and more than one of them added, "God bless you," in such a manner as to convince me that I had not made them angry, and that a sense of justice appeals to every nature.

At Edinburgh the hackman assured me that Darling's Hotel was full; every room was occupied. I had been warned by some of the strangers in the compartment not to believe what the hackmen said, and to avoid overcharges. I remembered the advice, and said, " I did not ask you whether there was room there.

I simply directed you to drive me there." At this he became not in the least angry, but repeated his assurance that the hotel was full. I was about to order a porter to change my box to another cab, when he said, " It was full yesterday ; but if you insist on it, I would as soon take you there as any place else." I did not believe him, in accordance with my previous instructions not to, and afterward learned that these fellows get a shilling from the proprietors of second-class houses for every guest they bring them. I paid the fellow the proper fee, which he took and then demanded more, saying that I had not given him enough. I did not believe him again, and was about to appeal the case to an officer, when he hastily drove away.

Darling's Hotel had several vacant rooms, and, having been located, I started out alone to see the city. I climbed up Calton Hill, without being aware of where I was going, and, in fact, without caring. If I had been in the keeping of some guide I could not have gone more wisely.

The reader who has stood on this eminence, an hour before sunset, of an autumn evening, need not be told that he has about him one of the most charming views afforded anywhere in Europe. Before you, and across the fairest portion of the city, is the castle, now occupied by Highland soldiers, who parade the streets in their kilts, with bare knees and tall caps. The beautiful gardens, on the steep hillside nearer you, are crowded with people. Lovers sit on the grassy slopes, and well-dressed, rollicking children play about them. Still nearer you, on the left of Princess Street, is the Walter Scott monument. This monument is a Gothic structure that rises from the corners of a square base by four great arches directed toward a common center, where a tower, gradually diminishing in size, reaches a height of two hundred feet. Above these arches are many pinnacles, which relieve the space and give symmetry to the monument. Beneath the archways is a statue of Scott, by the artist of Edinburgh, Sir John Steell. Within the niches are many statuettes of the characters described in the works of the poet and novelist. This monument, which has many rivals, but no superiors, is the conception of a practical mechanic, Mr. G. W. Kemp, whose name ought to be held in high regard by the city, and by all who look on his work. He was a man who, before this, had not gained any distinction, and critics, who were unwilling to see one rise to prominence who had not been under their patronage, began at once to belittle him. His work spoke for itself, and nothing could be said against it, for the splendid monument stood there to proclaim his praise. Then they said that he was not an inspired architect; that he was merely a copyist, and had gained his conceptions from a study of Melrose Abbey! But the claim is absurd, for there is nothing there from which such a copy could be made. It was not all original in the mind of the workman. He did not invent the Gothic style of architecture. But that was never invented by any man. All the great forms of architecture are copies from nature. God gave men models for everything in art, and he who takes from nature what is beautiful, and reproduces it in art, is not to be called a mere copyist. It is an inspiration; and he who gave forth the form of the Scott monument had this gift. No person ever saw it and afterward doubted whether the mental picture was of this or some other monument. There is no possibility of forgetting it, and no danger of the recollection not standing forth distinct from all else. Who that has seen the cathedral at Milan will ever have a confused idea of its appearance? In a cathedral there are many different parts to give it an individuality; but the monument has not this advantage; and yet this one erected to Walter Scott is unique in its every feature. It is absurd to claim that it is copied. As well might literary critics charge Sir Walter with plagiarism because he used the English language in his poems, as call the Scott monument a copy because of its Gothic architecture.

Near you on the hill are the ruins of an incomplete building. It was modeled after the Parthenon, and was intended to commemorate the bravery of the Scotch army; but as it is, it stands as a monument of Scotland's pride, and Scotland's poverty.

Beyond the limits of the city, and a little to the southeast, King Arthur's seat stands out boldly against the sky. Every royalist sees on this mountain the plain form of a lion resting his head on his fore paws, but to my Republican eyes there was no such image there.

In discovering mountain figures much depends on the vividness of the imagination and the lack of discrimination. The boy who said that, with certain things conceded, he could make a dog out of a stick of stovewood, was right.

"Imagine a dog's neck and head on one end of the stick, and a dog's tail on the other end, and the whole to be covered with hair, and then imagine four legs, with regular dog's paws attached to them, fastened on the under side of the stick, and you will have the prettiest dog you ever saw!"

If you will imagine enough of lacking details supplied, you can get a lion on the mountain. But it is this way the world over — we see what we want to see and are blind to beauties that we do not desire.

Turning a little to the left you see the Frith of Forth, or the river's outlet to the sea. But the sun is getting low, and we look almost toward it, just a little to the north, and behold Ben Ledi and Ben Lomond. I could not have seen them had the sun been in his mid-day strength; but as it was he seemed to be hovering above the mountain peaks, as though hesitating in his decision as to which mountain he would crown with gold. He smiled on both blushingly, refused to decide between the rivals, and sunk to rest a little south of them. Then you look back to man's work, down Princess Street with its palatial structures.

"What do you think of it?" asked a citizen, coming near me.

"Do you live here?" I asked in return, without answering his question.

"I do," he replied, "and I come up here every week to look again at this scene. But ye did na answer me."

"I think, sir," said I, "that this is one of the finest pictures made by the Great Artist, and one which, happily, you have not spoiled." As I said, this I looked at the Parthenonic failure and at the light-house-like monument to Nelson, and added, "any place except on this hill."

I retraced my steps to the hotel and sat down, for the second time in my life, at a public table where the guests are privileged to partake of food on which our Father's blessing has been publicly invoked. I formed the acquaintance of Mr. Varley, a business man of genial nature, who took me with him to Carrubbers' Close Mission Hall, where a large audience had assembled in the interests of Gospel temperance.

It is not always necessary to tell how little we know; there is one chance in ten that others may not discover our ignorance, if we maintain a discreet silence. I had heard of close corporations, but never in my life heard of a "close mission." We arrived at a narrow street; and in place of the mission being a close one, it was wide open. Gradually the light dawned on me that a close is a narrow street, and that the name of this street gives the name to the mission. How I missed the doctor now! He would have been so proud of me, that I had not displayed my ignorance but kept quiet, putting strangers to the trouble of discovering it for themselves! Why should I be so forward in giving information to those who have not asked for it? This mission is an eminently practical one, and is conducted by an eminently practical man, Mr. G. A. Barclay.

At ten o'clock the guests of the hotel, to the number of fifty, assembled in the parlors, and when they were seated the neatly-attired servants came in and took their seats. Miss Darling led in singing, a chapter of The Word was read, and on bended knee all united in a prayer to God, which seemed more earnest because it was offered up by those who had never met before, and they, guests in a hotel.

On the Sabbath I went with the family to hear Reverend John Smith. The services were pleasing to me, and Mr. Smith preached a sermon that was very able. It was, however, a little too profound. He gave theology to us just like the hotels serve bread in Europe — not in slices, as in America, but in great loaves, allowing each one to cut it for himself. It means work to listen to sermons that are so profound. I am told that in his off-hand discourses he breaks up the loaves in such a way that all who hear him get more than crumbs of comfort.

Men of great ability err in attempting to tell all that they have found out by a week of study, in a single discourse. It is possible to tell too much in too little time, and to tell it too profoundly. The sermon was one not to be forgotten, and its terse sentences rise in memory, like the thunderings of Elijah, or John the Baptist, many days after their utterance.

Monday morning I found at my plate a letter from Mr. Barclay, informing me that he had seen a friend of his, Mr. George Hastie, the former Curator of the

Antiquarian Museum, who would call shortly, and devote the day to me. Mr. Hastie is one of the best informed men I ever met. He is an enthusiast in antiquarian research. He is thoroughly posted in the history of Edinburgh, and to be that is to know the history of Scotland; and to know the history of Scotland is to be familiar with the history of Protestantism, for it is interwoven with that of Scotland. He took me in hand, and for nine hours led me through historic places, museums and galleries, churches and graveyards. Many of the places visited were closed; but when the guards saw my friend, they opened the doors to him. "Mr. Hastie, of the Antiquarian Museum!" was my " open sesame." But how ignorant I was! I had read Scott, and Burns, and Chalmers; I knew of Knox, and Queen Mary, and Lord Darnley, and felt myself able to talk a little about every one from Queen Margaret to Victoria. But Mr. Hastie took me into old ways, that to me were new. I sat in the corner where Burns talked to the widow, whom he visited secretly, and imagined that I could get occasional whiffs of his pipe, and saw him drinking his pot of ale as he made verses and recited them to Clarinda. But Mr. Hastie was proving that Burns was a Christian. Some of his poems plainly indicate that he was a firm believer. There is, however, an unfortunate difference between the theory and practice of Christianity.

Burns never claimed to be up to the proper standard.
But he did teach a charity that in a censorious world
is very beautiful :

> Then gently scan your brother man,
> Still gentler sister, woman ;
> Though they may gang a kennin' wrang,
> To step aside is human.

> One point must still be greatly dark,
> The moving, why they do it ;
> And just as lamely can you mark,
> How far, perhaps, they rue it.

> Who made the heart ! 'tis He alone,
> Decidedly can try us ;
> He knows each chord — its various tone,
> Each spring — its various bias.

> Then at the balance let's be mute,
> We never can adjust it ;
> What's done we partly may compute,
> But know not what's resisted.

No man ever took a firmer hold on the popular
heart than Burns. He hated hypocrisy, and had a
heart that was brimful of sympathy for the poor.
We are unwilling to allow Scotland to claim him ; he
belongs to us — to humanity.

The Antiquarian Museum was closed for the day;
but this was a kind providence, for it enabled me to
spend an hour and more with the former and present
curators. Cases were unlocked at my request, that

I might actually touch the precious things. I asked questions by the hundred, and received satisfactory answers to the most of them, although my inquisitiveness led me to ask some things that were unknowable. The curator read the hieroglyphics on monuments more easily than my friends read the hieroglyphics in my letters.

We visited the Cow Gate and Grass Market, where so many thousands were slain in the struggles of the Reformation. We, like others, went to Saint Giles' Church, and sat where Jennie Geddes sat, and handled the "cutty stool" which she threw at the clergyman's head when he attempted to read the collect, saying, "Do ye say mass in my lug?" She missed the preacher, but she struck prelacy a death-blow, and that was better than wounding the dean.

I climbed up into John Knox's pulpit, and thanked God for the Reformation; then turned to the "Solemn League and Covenant." The original parchment is neatly framed and signed; in some instances with blood, in place of ink. The question is being agitated whether the battles of the Reformation will have to be fought over again. The highest class of ritualism is found in England, and Rome boasts that it is not necessary for her to missionate in the Protestant church. Meantime, however, there are notes of warning sounded, and the church is casting about for a reformer, who shall come in the spirit and power of a Knox, and deliver her from the thraldom that is destroying her spiritual life.

Edinburgh is notably a city of monuments. Reformers, and statesmen, and poets, and writers, are remembered, and the young are taught to venerate the names of those who have made the land of Burns and Scott so favored. The beauty of the many statues is due to the genius of Sir John Steell. Everywhere you see his work.

"Where is Steell buried?" I asked of Mr. Hastie.

He said, "I will show you after a little." He pointed out in one of the old burying places a spot unmarked by any stone. I noticed it as strangely neglected. A thistle grows in the soft, rough ground, and weeds flourish beside the thistle.

"That," said Mr. Hastie, "is the grave of Sir John Steell."

It is a sad piece of neglect that no doubt will be, after a time, corrected. It is ungrateful to leave the grave of a man who did more than any other to beautify the city, without even a plain stone to mark the spot.

There is no part of Edinburgh more universally visited by strangers than the old Greyfriars, church-yard. To this yard three hundred cart-loads of human bones were conveyed when Saint Giles was remodeled.

16

They were deposited at the end of the church, and as no monument could be erected to the memory of the promiscuous and nameless dead, a bed of flowers was made over the spot. I walked about through the old grave-yard, looking at the monuments, and occasionally stopping to read the words on them, believing that the counsel in regard to the hackmen of Edinburgh might be applied to the epitaphs. The name and figures here were true, and, it may be, little else. But I came on one that struck me as original and I noted it down, only to discover next day that I could not find it again. But it was easy to remember. Some husband had prepared it for the tombstone of his wife:

> She was ———
> But words are wanting to tell what.
> Think what a wife should be,
> And she was that.

" Grand fellow ! " I said ; " what a splendid husband she must have had, or was he one of those mean mortals who only speak well of their wives when they are dead ? "

I had read but a little while before, on the tomb of the historian, Hume, the words, " Behold I come quickly." How little we know of the real character, either from obituary notices or epitaphs!

It is not generally known that in the noted old

church-yard, where so many martyrs are buried, and which is held in such high regard, a tomb has been found for a dog. Still less is it known that "Bobby" is buried in the flower-bed over the martyr bones brought from St. Giles. The history of "Bobby" is full of interest. His master died and was buried in the church-yard. "Bobby" went to the funeral, and unlike other mourners, refused to leave the grave. He stayed by it, and when driven away returned again. Near the entrance to the yard Mr. John Traill kept a coffee-house, and in him "Bobby" found a friend. Mr. Traill knew that the dog had refused to leave his master's grave, and made the acquaintance of the dog, seeking to win him away from his lonely watch by feeding him and taking him to his coffee-house. The dog appreciated his kindness and was a daily frequenter of Mr. Traill's place; but as soon as he had been fed he returned and stayed by the grave day and night. A stone had been placed above the grave, and under this "Bobby" found a resting place over his master's body. Mr. Traill made a bed for him there, but some people who regarded the dog's presence in the church-yard with disgust, lowered the stone to the ground and left "Bobby" without any protection. Then Mr. Traill was prosecuted for harboring the dog. The suit called attention to "Bobby's" fidelity, and also to the kindness of Mr. Traill, and then everybody was

willing to shelter the dog. But "Bobby" was true
to his friend, as he had been to his master, and daily
went to the coffee-house for his food. It may be that
the exposure to which he had been subjected told on his
health, but after about six years of watching "Bobby"
died, and was buried among the flowers. Lady Bur-
dette Coutts visited Edinburgh, and having heard the
story of "Bobby's" fidelity, erected a drinking ount-
ain on a public square, and above it placed a beautiful bronze statue of Greyfriars' 'Bobby'. I was so
much interested that I called to see Mr. Traill, whom
I found busy, serving coffee at a penny a cup. I
asked him about the dog, and he related his experience to me, with wonderful simplicity.

Then I said: "Mr. Traill, if you thought so much
of the dog, you ought to have saved him from his
persecutors. Why did you not own him, sir?"

Mr. Traill looked me straight in the face, and
said, with some little feeling: "I would gladly
have owned 'Bobby'; but, sir, 'Bobby' would not
own me!"

I gave the honest fellow my hand, and said: "You
have been kind to the dog. God bless the man who
is kind to a dog! But will you be kind to —" He
seemed to think I wanted him to be kind to me,
and was evidently about to offer me a cup of coffee;
but I added, "be kind to yourself!"

For the first time I realized that in this humble person I was speaking to a man greater than his calling.

His answer was : " I believe in Jesus and the resurrection ! "

It may be that Mr. Traill's interest was due to a perusal of " Rob and His Friends," by one of Scotland's most noted men.

It is worthy of record, that savage tribes which kept dogs never became cannibals.

CHAPTER XVI.

HOLYROOD PALACE is an unpretentious building, in a part of the city that is destitute of beauty. Occasionally Queen Victoria honors it with a visit, and finds that it is kept in good repair by servants, whose duty it is to see that all is ready, for the Queen may visit the palace once in five, or ten, or twenty years.

But while the building itself is destitute of architectural beauty, it has, to the tourist, a wealth of historical associations. The apartments of Queen Mary are very interesting. The bed that belonged to the unhappy Queen is as she left it, except the changes made on it by the lapse of years. The silk covering is decaying, and will, after awhile, fall to pieces. Her work-box is not now opened to the public, for many tourists have proven themselves rather skillful shop-lifters, and the precious things might be scattered abroad. But, through the special favor of Mr. Hastie, the box was opened, and I was permitted to rummage through it at will. There is an elegant specimen of embroidery on the inner lid, representing Jacob's vision at Bethel. If the foot of the ladder reached to the unfortunate Mary, it must have been down in some low valley, for her sorrows were great.

The ordinary keeper, or guide, would have resolutely affirmed that the little tear-bottle belonged to Mary, and that the stains on the glass were the saline deposits from the eyes of the beautiful Queen. This is a tear-bottle, but Mary may never have seen it. I do not think it would have been large enough for her. She would have filled a half-dozen bottles of this size, any day, after having a little unpleasantness with Lord Darnley.

I do not understand how the Queen of England can sleep well at Holyrood. She certainly does not believe in spooks, or she would hear cries and see all sorts of hobgoblins in her dreams. A creepy feeling comes over one of sensitive nature, when in rooms where crimes have been committed.

I do not wonder that Mary did not love Darnley, though he had those qualities that make some men lovely in the eyes of a few women. But he was jealous of the Queen's secretary—the Italian, Rizzio. In the room which we have entered, the Queen was sitting when Darnley came in, and, dropping down beside her, clasped her in his arms. He was not wont to exhibit such marks of affection in the presence of her secretary. But the secret of the demonstration was soon disclosed by the band of hired murderers, who followed him and attacked the frightened Rizzio. The latter ran behind the Queen, grasped her dress, and piteously begged for his life. Reaching over the royal person of his Queen, the assassin struck the fatal blow, and the Queen's vestures were stained with the secretary's blood. Then he was dragged from the room, and brutally slain. How could she love this man after such an act? These walls have shut in many a sad secret from the world, listening outside. She had contemplated a divorce, but Darnley took sick, no doubt caused by his tumultuous experiences, the raging passions and terrible remorse that must have preyed on his heart. Queen Mary seems to have been softened by his sickness, and the weak fellow received her assiduous attentions. Whether he improved much under her care, is not known; but her love, if it were ever rekindled to him, did not burn very brightly.

Darnley lived in a house by himself. This house was blown up and he was killed. The Queen was suspected with having been privy to the plot. He was only in name her husband, and it is manifest that if she used a tear-bottle, the little one I handled would have been too large for the occasion.

Bothwell was suspected of having something to do

with blowing up Darnley, but the suspicions were not generally entertained. It was hard to think that he would kill a husband in order to marry the widow, when by the laws of society he would be compelled to wait several years before forming the new tie. But the suspicion became a conviction, when Mary's sorrows were completely drowned, and she had her bark ready for another matrimonial sail three months after her husband's death. This marriage so outraged the public mind that she and Bothwell were believed to be murderers; and the accusation was openly made. An insurrection followed. Bothwell fled, and Mary was imprisoned. With the rest of her sad history the reader is familiar. Fleeing to England, she was again made a prisoner, and after eighteen years was executed. Her body was buried in Westminster.

But to return to the work-box. I was examining the tear-bottle, and trying on Mary's thimble and criticising her embroidery, and wondering where all the patches came from, and why she did not keep things in better order, when I ran off into this page of history.

The keeper seemed pleased to know me. I was an exceptionally fine visitor. I had not put the bottle in my pocket, nor stolen the thimble, nor cut a round or two out of the ladder, nor smuggled some of the patchwork.

Then I asked him if there was anything else about the room that was kept from the public gaze. There is generally some dark closet or stowaway place where old things are kept for the charity society or the rag- man. I was right. He had just such a nook for old boots and hats and things.

"Yes, we used to show Lord Darnley's boot, but we have refused to let visitors see it at all now."

"Why?"

"If you saw the boot, you would know the reason."

"Then, suppose you let me see it, that I may find out for myself."

I was very anxious now to see the boot, since it was not exhibited. It is always that way with us. For- bidden fruit is sweet. The fish that got away from the hook just as you were about to land it was larger than any you had in your basket. The unattainable good is better than that which is freely offered us. The boot was produced. It did not look much like the patent-leather variety worn by the modern fas- tidious youth; and yet Darnley was a fop. It was square-toed, and had on the top of it an adjustable piece that must have been intended for kneeling on when Darnley was out grouse hunting. It was in a good state of preservation, except that the relic- gatherers had cut away a large piece near the top of the instep. I might have tried it on, but I was not the least anxious to stand in his shoes.

The house of John Knox remains, substantially, as it was when the great reformer lived in it. A stone in the street, with the letters " J. K." engraved on it, is the supposed spot where his body lies buried. But it is intimated that there is no certainty about this, and that what was said about Moses may be said of Knox: "Of his sepulcher knoweth no man." But it is convenient to believe that the stone is directly over the body, and the old argument might be applied to this question: If he is not buried there, where is he buried?

The castle, to one who has not seen others somewhat like this one, will be an object of great interest. The regalia of Scotland's chiefs, with crowns, scepters, swords, and other curiosities of kingly and queenly attire, are securely guarded in the crown-room.

Mons Meg, a great cannon four hundred years old, but now entirely harmless, lies in state in front of Saint Margaret's chapel. Where the cannon came from is a matter of dispute. Some assert that it was brought from Belgium; but the more popular belief is that it was made by a certain blacksmith, of Castle Douglas, who named it Meg, in honor of his wife. If the gun suggested the wife, it would have been a wise precaution, even for a stout blacksmith, to have kept the peace with her; or else, before giving battle, to have sent an embassage and made the best possible terms. The cannon was kept for a hundred and fifty years in the Tower at London, but was at last restored, and dragged up the castle hill by horses and patriotic citizens. Mr. Hastie exercised himself, with others, in this enterprise.

Guides have informed tourists that a cannon ball, partly buried in the Tower, was shot there by Cromwell, and it is looked at in wonder and credulity. It was placed there to mark the water level of the reservoir on a hill near by. The regular guide tells so many lies that he believes them himself after awhile, and delights to excite the wonder of strangers.

Edinburgh is not inappropriately called "Modern Athens" by her people. Her educational and charitable institutions are famed throughout the world, and the pleasing views afforded, either from Calton Hill or the castle, are not excelled anywhere in Europe. But I can not forget the Cow Gate and Grass Market; the miserable displays of rags and wretchedness; the drunkenness and revelings in the low parts of the city. I have never seen so many drunken women in any other city. How many poor women reel along the low streets, or lie every night in the gutters! If Jesus could have seen this city, that bears so many monuments of Scotland's glory, He would have wept

over it. And yet so dominant is the temperance sentiment in Scotland, that had she the right to make
her own laws, she would banish the saloon forever;
but the English government will not permit this sort
of home rule, and so the curse of the liquor traffic
rests on a loyal people. Many are the sins that lie at
the doors of the mighty, and the fields of yellow
barley and bright poppy bear witness to a nation's
greed. Is not England rich enough without traffick-
ing in opium and rum? But it becomes us, in regard
to the latter, to think of America.

It would have been a mark of disloyalty to Scotland
not to visit Abbotsford, the home of Sir Walter Scott.
The ride from Edinburgh is a short one, and the drive
to the Scott mansion is pleasant. The house, however, is much like the astronomer's garden : It fails to
reveal the secret of lofty meditations. It gave me
no inspiration whatever to sit in his chair or look at
his books. I was as barren of verse when I did this
as ever in my life. But when you are shown the
relics that Sir Walter had collected about him—the
sword of Roderick Dhu, and some of the trappings
of Fitz James, and the knife of Rob Roy—there is
some stirring of the spirit. The guardian of the
treasures looked at me with amazement, or contempt,
I do not know which, when I asked what great things
Messrs. Dhu and Roy had done, that the old knives

they used should be regarded so highly? He asked me if I had not read Sir Walter's poems, or knew nothing of the stories of the Highlands? But yet he was not able to tell me just what they had done that was worthy writing and singing about, and why their old swords and hunting knives should be kept so sacredly.

Melrose Abbey presents some of the finest work in architecture that you will find anywhere. The Abbey has been subjected to the despoiler, and but a small portion of it remains. It is said that the heart of Bruce is buried within its walls. The part of the structure that interested me was the outside of the walls, on which there remain traces of most beautiful sculpture. The chisel that executed this work was not held in any ordinary hand; but, alas! like much of man's work, its beauty has been marred by the very service to which it was put, and by the hands that were determined to destroy because of political or religious zeal.

Once more I determined to get away from man's work to God's, and taking a last look at beautiful Edinburgh, started on the varied trip to Calendar, the Trossachs, and lakes; varied, because it is in part by steam car, in part by omnibus, in part by boat, and you can walk to your heart's content.

It is peculiar how careless some travelers become.

A gentleman and his wife, whom we had frequently met on the continent, had bought tickets to Calendar; but when they met agreeable companions, in the persons of Dr. and Mrs. J. L. Robinson, they determined to go with them as far as they could. When we came to Calendar, they said to the agent: "We do not wish to go to Glasgow, but want to go with our friends, through the Trossachs and by the lakes."

"Then I will sell you a ticket to Cragin-Doran," said the agent.

The ticket was purchased, but not one of us had the least idea where Cragin-Doran was, and the party who had purchased cared as little as he knew. He had time on his hands, and had a ticket in his pocket for Cragin-Doran, and he was happy.

When the conversation would lag on other subjects we would always enliven it by asking :

"Mr. Carpenter, pray tell us where is Cragin-Doran?"

It became a little monotonous after awhile, but Mr. Carpenter was too much of a gentleman to show the least annoyance.

The Trossachs is the "bristly country," and is so called because of the thick growth of wood, mostly birch and oak, that abounds there. Every part of the route is rendered immortal by the poems of Scott. The mountain side, where at last his "gallant gray lay dying," would not be interesting at all were it not for the way he has brought it out in his inimitable "Lady of the Lake."

Coilantogle Ford is a canal of the Glasgow Water-Works. It is rather hard on the fancies of poetry, but does not interfere with its facts, to make historic places part of a useful system for supplying the needs of a great city.

We had expected great things of Loch Katrine, and our anticipations were realized. Its entrance is by a very narrow way, described by the poet as affording scanty room for the brood of the wild duck to swim in to the broader waters. The mountains rise in rugged beauty above you, and in this narrow way you feel the power of nature to awaken feelings of delight.

"Ellen's Isle" is but a little rocky spot that contains, possibly, three acres. It was a secure resting place, and Ellen's harp and song would have sounded very sweetly to the tired hunter. The place is suggestive of that solitude where the soldier or the huntsman may rest without fear of being disturbed by the blast of bugle or beat of drum.

> Huntsman rest ! thy chase is done,
>> While our slumb'rous spells assail ye ;
> Dream not with the rising sun,
>> Bugles here shall sound reveillé.

Sleep ! the deer is in his den ;
   Sleep ! thy hounds are by thee lying ;
Sleep ! nor dream in yonder glen
   How thy gallant steed lay dying.

Huntsman, rest ! thy chase is done ;
   Think not of the rising sun,
For at dawning to assail ye,
   Here no bugles sound reveillé.

A thousand beauties may be seen from Loch Lomond, including the islands of the lake itself; the mountains that surround it; the cascades that start out from among the ferns and heather, like frightened animals, only that they come toward you; the pretty little villages that sit near the shore, like flocks of water-fowl resting their wings.

We look on Ben Lomond and recall the song, heard so often in childhood:

The sun has gane down o'er the lofty Ben Lomond,
   And left the red clouds to preside o'er the scene,
While lanely I stray in the calm simmer gloamin'
   To muse on sweet Jessie, the flower o' Dumblane.

Jessie did not put in her appearance when I was in Dumblane, and it is possible that her descendants have not inherited her beauty.

But I shall always remember the lake and mountain, because of a picture painted there for us by the

17

Great Artist. It was raining a little betimes during the entire day, and the showers were broken off by brilliant bursts of sunlight that gave false promise of constancy. It was a struggle between sun and shower. Looking out toward Ben Lomond, where the clouds were hanging, a beautiful bow appeared. It was formed at first against the cloud, and was not remarkable in appearance; but as it extended down to the water's edge, the mountain, and not the cloud, became the background. I had never seen a rainbow anywhere, except against the cloud; but here the bow was against the green mountain, and this was continued even into the lake. Up to within a few yards of the boat, the bow was distinctly visible, with the waters of Loch Lomond for a background. " Behold, I set my bow in the clouds! " was the language addressed to Noah, but here the bow was set on the mountain side, and on the lake, and both lake and mountain had new glories not painted by human hands.

When we had entered the train for Glasgow the guard courteously informed Mr. Carpenter that he must change at some station, which he named, for Cragin-Doran; but somehow he had concluded now to go on with us to Glasgow, and he never was permitted to see the town to which he had bought his ticket. This happy-go-easy way of traveling may seem strange to those who always have business taking them from

one place to another. But why might we not as well-
have gone to Cragin-Doran as any place else?

Rothesay, on the Isle of Bute, is one of the petti-
est places I have ever visited. The town lies in the
center of a shore crescent, and every part of it can be
seen as you enter. The first suggestion to my mind
was that the shore was stretching forth its arms ready
to clasp the inland sea to its bosom. I was com-
mended to the hospitable home of Mr. Milloy, whose
name is near enough my own to claim some kinship.
I assured him that I could only remain a few hours,
and then he said I must never leave without seeing
the "Kyles of Bute." "We will take a look at the
old castle, and then get the steamer and go out for a
four hours' ride and come back to dinner, and you can
still get the evening boat for Gurnock."

Another old castle! They are everywhere! What
business has an old castle in beautiful Rothesay?

But it is here, nevertheless. I walked through the
castle and saw the great fire-place where an ox could
be roasted at one time, and looked at the moat and
the portcullis, and then to the boat landing. But
I was lost, completely lost. I did not know what to
make out of my friend's suggestion, that we visit the
"Kyles of Bute." I was too impatient to wait for
an explanation, and determined to be honest. I began
mildly :

"Kindly tell me why they call this island *Bute* ?"

"I suppose because it is somewhat the shape of a boot."

"But what are the kyles ?"

"You will soon see. The channels become so narrow that you will hardly see how to get out of them."

"O! Mr. Milloy, I see it now! The island of Bute is the shape of a boot and the kyles are the narrows!"

Why did I not keep quiet, and wait till I found out for myself? I wondered if Mr. Milloy would not be ashamed of the stupidity of Mr. Meloy. But I was relieved when I discovered that in introducing me to a number of gentlemen, who were his friends, he did not tell them that my name had an "e" in it, in place of an "i," and that, therefore, we were not related. I breathed more freely now and began at once talking to the gentlemen about the beauty of the kyles, as though I had always known the meaning of the term. I saw that Mr. Milloy was proud of his relative, only when I made a dozen stupid blunders, which he corrected for me with so much skill that it was difficult to tell that I had made them. But as he did it I could see a merry twinkle in his eye. How jealous the doctor would have been of my knowledge, had he been along; but he was handling a scalpel in a London hospital.

On a sloping hill-side, Colonel Campbell, after his

return from Waterloo, determined to make a living memorial of the battle. He had the position of the troops carefully laid out, and then planted trees, whose foliage was of different shades, to represent the various divisions of the armies engaged in the conflict. It was a splendid conception, and was carried out so fully that the forest planted by him, giving a picture of Waterloo, was famed far and near. But even art in living wood dies out, and the trees began to fade, and the ranks of living green, like the ranks of the old warriors, were soon broken, and to-day but a few hardy old trees stand here and there, on the hill-side, without any seeming arrangement. How like the veterans of our war! The ranks are broken, and soon but a few old men will be left to tell of a great army, once so full of life, and hope, and courage. The forest picture has nearly faded away.

In a substantial-looking house, on the island, one of the family of inventors — the Stevensons — lives. He is now a very old man, and employs his time in carving ivory. His work is said to excel that of the orientals, and he employs the hours of life's evening in this simple way.

After a sumptuous meal, at the elegant home of Mr. Milloy, I boarded a steamer that was crowded with excursionists, mostly from Glasgow. To my surprise and delight, I saw the friends who had been with me on the lakes seated together, earnestly talk-ing. They had heard that I had taken sick in some hotel in Glasgow. The last person that had listened to my voice said I was sick; but I was talking to her through a telephone. That always makes me feel ill, and sometimes talk the same way. It was cruel to bring it up again, but I said: "I am so glad to meet you! I thought Mr. Carpenter had gone to Cragin-Doran!" We had a delightful evening together in Glasgow, and parted in the night, to meet, it may be, only on the other shore, in the brightness of the morning whose day shall know no clouds.

Early next morning, I left the sleeping city of Glas-gow, and at ten o'clock, from Paddy's Mile-Stone, looked back to the land whose noble martyrs saved to England, and it may be to the world, the sublime tenets of the Christian faith.

CHAPTER XVII

IT is not strange that Ireland is called the "Green Isle." It could not well be anything else, either in name or reality. It rains and drizzles day after day, sprinkling hills and valleys, and allowing the sun to take only an occasional look at one of the prettiest spots on earth. Little fields surrounded by hedges, and dividing the land into all sorts of odd-shaped patches, may not be convenient to the farmer, but they have a charm for the lovers of art. The land subdivisions do not indicate the use of the square and compass, and there is a seeming disorder about them that is refreshing. They remind one of a parlor after a lot of rollicking boys have beenin it for an hour. It may be very untidy, but it does not look stiff. There is nothing in these fields that suggests a checker-board.

It is the middle of September, and the oats and grass are not yet harvested. It is cold and damp, and we draw up near the turf fire and rub our hands in joy because we have felt the heat. Women are in the fields between showers, turning over the little lap bunches with their hands. It is slow work, but it is the only way that hay can be cured in Ireland. I went out among them, and they seemed happy and contented.

A number of women were making calls on their neighbors, and, in place of sitting with pearl or gold card-cases in their hands, they all went out to the fields to earn a few pennies by an afternoon's work. It takes more labor to harvest one acre of grass in Ireland, than it does to put up forty acres in America. Hay sells at about the same price in Belfast that it does in Chicago. It may therefore be seen that the wages paid must be exceedingly small. The land tenant or owner can not possibly pay the prices that we pay in this country for labor. A good man boards himself and receives from seven to ten shillings a week. I saw two honest-looking fellows at work, who had been in the same man's employ for fourteen years, and they received every Saturday seven shillings — one dollar and sixty-eight cents — for their week's work. These men pay a shilling or two a month for their little houses (about all they are worth), clothe themselves and their families, and have something laid up in bank. Their wives occasionally turn in and earn a little money, which is so much gained. They live on oatmeal and milk, with an occasional piece of meat, which is esteemed a luxury not to be eaten too frequently. If the Irish people who have come to America practiced the same economy here that they did in Ireland, they would soon own the country. But we have demonstrated the fact that high wages do not make contented workmen.

I admire the jaunting car, and disgust the more aristocratic cabmen by always calling for a car. It has often been described, but I had no idea what it was like until I climbed up on it, and thought I would fall down from it!

It is a cart, in the front of which the driver sits, and four passengers ride sideways, two on a side, with their feet extending out beyond and over the wheels, Choose your partners, for you must keep your backs to the backs of the other two; and if the driver is swinging round a corner, which he is liable to do without provocation, it may be well that you have confined your conversation to your own partner.

As we come near Belfast, Carrick Fergus is seen a little to the north. It has an old castle, once very strong, and still fortified, and a community of Scotch, the descendants of a colony driven from home by religious persecution in the seventeenth century. But Carrick Fergus is best remembered as the place where William III. landed, and from which he pressed on against the forces of James II., defeating his father-in-law, who had for years been plotting to make his daughter a widow! William had married into a rather tough family; but then we must always pay due veneration to royalty. Kinship counts for nothing among those who may wear crowns, if the countries to which it belongs are not on amicable terms. But England and the world owe a debt of gratitude to William; for had the battle been decided against the descendant of the House of Orange, the inquisition would have been at work in England, and the world would have gone backward farther in years than the shadow of the sun did in degrees, by the dial of Ahaz.

I was anxious to get away from Belfast, to see something of the more rural life of the Irish people. Armagh is a country town, where the people come to do their marketing. The streets were filled with horses, and cars, and carts. Aside from the difference in the appearance of the vehicles, one might have imagined that he was in a town in one of our older States on a Saturday afternoon, when every hitching-post is occupied and country produce is being exchanged for groceries and dry goods. Thomas Hall, Esquire, of Loch Gall, came to meet me and took me to his home, where I spent the Sabbath. Here I had the opportunity of testing the size of an Irish gentleman's heart, and I discovered that it was as large as I had always believed it to be. His liveried coachman knew the road to perfection, and the fine-stepping horse he drove, took the bit and made the six-mile drive seem very short. The homestead was once called "Eden;" but Mr. Hall divided it, and called the part he retained for himself "Cloven Eden." If beautiful trees of fruitage and shade, well-kept lawns, and bright flowers, yea, and a river flowing through it, were types of the old Eden, they certainly distinguish the new. We strolled over the farm and discussed agriculture and politics. It sounded strange to my Western ears to hear oats called "corn," and to be in a country where our Indian corn is not seen.

On the Sabbath I tried to preach in the church of Rev. Mr. Smith, a man of great intellectual power and benevolent nature. He is an exception among clergymen, having a little superabundance of this world's treasures, which he wisely distributes among the poor of his parish and neighborhood. Many a load of turf is laid down at the doors of the poor which should be credited to the pastor.

The turf is found wherever there has been a decay of vegetable life. Under greater pressure it would have become coal. It is found principally in the low lands, but is also obtained in the mountains, where there are dishes in the rocks. After being cut out, it is stacked up in such a way that the air passes freely between

the pieces, and is thus thoroughly dried, when it is
ready to be burned. In a mild climate it makes sufficient heat, but in our rigid winters would hardly keep
us from shivering. It may never be exhausted; but if
it should be, there will no doubt be something to take
its place.

It is comparatively but a short time since many
looked with alarm on the destruction of the American
forests, and complained when the solid oak or tall
hickory, on whose topmost branches the squirrel chat-
tered to his mate, fell by the blow of the woodman's
axe. "What will the next generation do without
wood?" Then the black diamonds were uncovered
and the vast coal fields gave up their treasures. A
younger man said: "At the present rate of consumption the coal will soon be burned, and the coming
generations will suffer because of our prodigality!"
But now, if we visit the old homestead, we will find
neither wood-pile nor coal-bin, while age sits beside
the glowing fires of natural gas. The same alarm
holds good in regard to the stories of this being
exhausted. It is well for us to use the blessings
that we have, and not worry too much about future
generations that will not be grateful for our economy.
I left the delightful family circle of Mr. Hall, not
wondering that there was to him and his "no place
like home."

On the way to Dublin, the double compartment was filled with mill hands going to hear Mr. Moody. They sang as they journeyed, from the Moody and Sankey books, not very sweetly but with emphasis. At Dublin I found Doctor Davis waiting for me at the Shelbourne. We had mutual confessions to make of our doings while separated, and the two weeks seemed more than fourteen days to us.

I took a drive through the city and then out through Phœnix Park, which contains nearly two thousand acres. In this park, in the year 1800, a duel was fought between Grattan and Corry. It was during the last session of the Irish Parliament, and the day after Grattan had made a speech, that was for many years considered a model of parliamentary severity. He showed how much a man can say without violating the laws of debate. " I will not call him villain, because it would be unparliamentary, and he is a privy councilor. I will not call him fool, because he happens to be chancellor of the exchequer." Corry challenged him, it may be because he did not call him a fool and a villain. Corry showed himself to be the former by making a challenge, and Grattan revealed himself to be a brother of the order by accepting it. The sheriff somehow had become aware of the time and place of meeting. He was there to interfere, but had no *posse* with him. General Craddock, Corry's second, threw the officer of the law in a ditch, and held him there while the duel proceeded. At the first fire, Corry was wounded in the arm. The second shot Grattan fired in the air, and Corry was too much excited to take sure aim. The ridiculous occurrence was made much of at the time, but the real hero of the occasion was the brave Craddock, who held the sheriff down in the ditch.

The spot where Burke and Cavendish were murdered a few years ago was pointed out. There is, however, nothing new under the sun. The flowers, and greensward, and boulevards, have counterparts in parks, which you have seen in America.

The only thing different to me was the deer that feed without fear, and remain in the park without being fenced in. They are as tame as sheep. If we were kind to wild beasts and birds, they would be gentle and tame. Years of human savagery have made them fearful of us. Man's sway over the lower orders of creation will be complete only when he has learned the law of kindness. The little child will *lead*, not drive the wolf, and lion, and bear. Society may be elevated without the thumb-screw, or iron collar, or gloomy dungeon. Gradually the world is coming forward to recognize a new king, who is omnipotent—

I have again been disappointed in the south of Ireland. The road from Dublin to Killarney does not awaken painful reflections of the people's poverty. Green fields, where sheep and fatted cattle graze; houses with thatched roofs, but with whitewashed walls; flowers peeping through windows, tell us of substantial comforts, if not of luxury. I know that there may be a great lack of tidiness, even where roses bloom! In some places the "chickens come home to roost" behind the doors, and the calf is not put to bed with the children, but is tied to the bedpost! If one is inclined to be æsthetic, he will discover many things, even in America, that will be in some degree offensive.

But where are the people? I had always supposed that Ireland was like a scattered village, and that farm-houses were to be seen close to each other, and that the lanes were filled with children. This is a great mistake, for you will go miles without seeing a man, woman, or child, on the highways. Ireland is in America! Chicago has two hundred and fifteen thousand of the children of the "Green Isle" in her population, while New York has a larger number. If the people will be patient, the landlord problem will solve itself. I talked with a linen manufacturer, who told me that some of his mills were closed because the American kitchen paid higher wages than the Belfast loom.

It is not safe, when taking the tour of Europe, to

stop at Queenstown and visit Killarney, and it is not wise to go to Liverpool and leave off the visit to Killarney until you are coming home. In the first, the danger is that you will be so much delighted that you will say, "Killarney is good enough for me; I do not care to see any other place;" in the second way, you are liable to say, "I have seen so much, and there is nothing of interest in Ireland; I will go directly home." It was only because we had solemnly promised not to leave off the southern lakes of Ireland that we timed ourselves to be there. I shall never cease to be thankful that we took the Prince of Wales Road from Killarney to Bantry. It used to be said, "See Rome and die;" but I would advise my friends, "See Killarney and live!" for, ever in your after life, there will be in your mind a picture, whose richness and lovely tints, and bold perspective, will come before you, giving a charm to solitude, as you call it. We are so much afraid of long distance rides by diligence in this country that there is danger of our turning away from Killarney to reach Cork by rail. The route overland by carriage is forty-seven miles to Glengariff, and eight miles from there to Bantry, where you take the cars for Cork. But the regret will be that the ride to Glengariff is so short. The omnibus provides nothing but outside seats, so that the landscape can be enjoyed to the full. There is here a richer variety of scenery than can be

THE LAKES OF KILLARNEY.

found in such combinations any place else in the world. The road is now up the mountain side and through tunnels in projecting rocks, and again on the heights, where you can look down on the valleys and lakes; and anon by the sides of the lakes, under leafy boughs, where the mystic greenery of the fern blends with the leaves of oak and beech. We have frequent glimpses of mountain streamlets rising from the heath and bracken and leaping down the mountain sides, to mingle their waters with the Killarney lakes. There are lakes far above you, hedged in by rims of solid rock, whose waters drip over the brims like the waters from an overflowing cup. Here and there you pass old stone houses with thatched roofs and stables close by them. Barefooted children are about the low doors, and every feature of the face, and every flag on the hallways, indicates a scarcity of soap and water. But these are offset by vine-clad cottages surrounded by flowers. Ferns, with their delicate leaves, fringe the roadway and reach over the banks above you, as though to wave a welcome. The limbs of many of the oaks are covered several inches thick with moss, and in this moss the ferns have taken root and grown with their long, waving branches spreading down on both sides of the limbs. Look more carefully, and to the very uppermost branches of the trees the ferns are growing. The picture is

18

fairer than could be painted ; the scene is more refreshing than could have been prepared by the skill of
human hands. The oak tree alone would be pretty; but
the oak tree covered with moss, and in the moss delicate leaved ferns, seems like fairy land. The branches
that interlace over the roadway enable you to pass
through verdant bowers. One might grow weary of
verdure ; and, as if to relieve this, the delicate heather
and its gayer sister, the heath, lend their aid.

When, however, you have passed the summit, and
entered the County of Cork, and the wide valleys
above Bantry Bay appear, that which before was
pleasing becomes enchanting. At each turn of the
road a fresh surprise awaits you. The far-off mountain tops are hooded with storms ; the mountain sides
are ribbed, and studded with rocks ; great slopes,
reaching down toward the valley, are clad with heath
and bracken. Irregular fields of grain are on the
lower slopes, and now you see many a score of laugh-
ing streams gleefully leaving the heights, like happy
children off for a holiday. But this is only a little of
it all. Light and shade play important parts in this
picture. The sky is filled with clouds ; not one great
dull coating for the whole, but a thousand small
clouds, that float between different parts of the view
and the sun. The patches of sunshine on mountain

slope, or valley, or about your way, appear like winged birds eagerly pursuing each other in their flight.

You have seen the photographer adjusting the curtains of his gallery so as to secure the right proportions of light and shade. The Great Artist, knowing that some of his children were looking on this for the last time, folded up and again spread out the curtains of the sky to glorify the landscape. He has been kind and considerate in other ways, and why not favor us now?

I wrote these words on the evening after the journey, with the scenes still fresh in my mind, but with a feeling of regret that my pen was too feeble to express the emotions of my soul. The picture is on my heart; but I have looked on the poor art that seeks to portray it much as a parent might look on the picture of a departed child. Where are the smiles? Where the expression of the eye? Where is the soul that looked through the windows? Where is the gloss of the hair, and the arched simplicity of the brow? Where is the dew that was on the lips, and the rosy tints on cheeks and fingers? Alas! there is no art to reproduce these; they belonged to the life within, and it is gone. So, as I read these words, I am pleased that there is a resemblance; they give a faint idea of the glory revealed; but along with this I have pity for the weakness of the artist, and profound regret that, no matter how skilled one may be, the picture can never be reproduced as I have seen it. Every sketch of the purple hills, whether by pen or brush, has disappointed.

Not one tourist in a hundred ever takes this delight-ful ride, because it has not been advertised as other parts of Europe have been. But there is another reason, even more potent than this. The pen of the novelist, or poet, has not given to lakes and mountain passes the charm of some fascinating romance. The southern part of Ireland has not produced those types of intellectual splendor that render the land of Scott and Burns so famous. It is not because the Irishman's intellect is deficient in natural vigor, or his powers of description are limited, for no people excel him in these respects. The reason must be looked for elsewhere, and may be found in an unfortunate and oppressive system of religious dogmatism, that has sought to take away the key of knowledge from the people, and in so doing has impoverished a once fertile land, leaving it in barrenness. Religious tyranny always reacts. A gifted writer, to have thrown the spell of a story about Killarney, or Glengariff, or the Gap of Dunlow, would have brought tourists by the thousand, to look on the beauties that stupidity and bigotry have been unable to reveal. If the world is yet in its youth, the error may be corrected; but it will take centuries to awaken an interest in a land that has been contented with the legends of Saint Patrick.

Cork has so often been spoken of with ridicule that I was not prepared to see a city of so much importance and such business enterprise. It is the third city in Ireland, and has wide streets, elegant stores, and a general look of prosperity. If it were not for the depopulation of Ireland, Cork would be a very progressive and prosperous city. A considerable garrison of soldiers is kept here, and I suppose that it may as well be kept in Cork as any place else. Two of these soldiers were in a compartment with us, two days before reaching Cork. One of them was a sergeant and seemed to feel the importance of his position. His companion was only a private soldier and kept the bottle of poteen ready at his call. A young Irish mother was also in the compartment, with a babe about one year old. The soldiers gave her the bottle, and she frequently put it to her lips, feeling great respect for the red coats of the British army. She even took the bottle and wet the lips of her child with its contents, and this so much delighted the idiotic sergeant that he asked her for the babe and amused it between drinks, to the great delight of the mother. It would have been a good place for a temperance lecture if the pearls would not have been trampled under the soldier's feet. The sergeant became a little more hilarious and told the mother that he would toss her baby out of the car window. I was not sure but that it might be the best thing that could happen the child. Then he took it in his hands and laughingly held it out through the window, threatening to let it drop. At this she became somewhat alarmed, but really the babe was in more deadly peril when she was giving it whisky.

Great preparations were made to hear Mr. Moody, and a building used for a circus was made ready for the congregation. I had a desire to hear him in Cork, and to know what sort of an audience he would attract. There was a crowd on the streets long before the hour for opening the house. Every part of the building was packed full and Mr. Moody preached the same simple Gospel that he does at home. There is a very large Protestant population in Cork, and this was fully represented; but there were hundreds of Catholics eager to hear the Evangelist. It was the only time that I ever knew Mr. Moody to be confronted by an audience, many of whom were not in sympathy with him, and came there simply to jeer. He was equal to the occasion, however, and held them in control until his sermon was ended. Then he called for individual requests and confessions. Some of the audience began to laugh at each word spoken, if there was anything in

the voice or manner that could possibly be ridiculed.
Mr. Moody waxed bold, and talked like Paul did to
Elymas. He did not call them "children of the
devil," but he did talk so directly to them that they
wilted under his rebuke, and then he requested them
to leave the house, or else remain in it with a better
spirit. The meeting was his, and he proposed to conduct it, and he did. Many professed conversion, and
among them several soldiers rose for prayers. I do
not think that the men who tried to interrupt Mr.
Moody's meeting would make another effort in that
direction.

CHAPTER XVIII.

E had jested about buying the Blarney Stone and bringing it to Chicago. Some of the more ignorant people supposed that we were in earnest, and it was even hinted that the entire castle might be taken to the World's Fair. They have heard such exaggerated stories about what Americans will do that nothing seems to stagger them. We engaged an enterprising artist (Mr. Guy) to go out with us to the castle, and take a character picture of the scene that would, in all probability, occur if we made the attempt to carry out our plans. A delightful ride of five miles in a jaunting car brought us to the castle. The doctor had gone out by the train and I had ordered my favorite car. When in sight of the castle, I saw my friend on the highest wall, waving his hat. He was where in other times he could not have gone without an army and without serious fighting. But now there was nothing to oppose him. The gate to the castle is closed to all who have not paid a shilling to see it. The grounds are in the possession of Lord (no matter about his name), who gathers in a considerable sum from visitors. One might have heard some excited people talking:

" Och, sure, and you need not be fearin' that; they niver could get it away."

" Don't be too sartin of that. The Chicaggy people brought a whole prison to their wicked citty without ever disturbin' a brick, or scalin' off a bit of the plaster. They have the idintical hole through which their soldiers got out, and are gathering in shillings for allowing people to look into it."

We obtained a fine picture of the castle for the *Illustrated World's Fair*, with Doctor Davis in the act of negotiating for the stone. Mr. Rose-Cleland, a manufacturer of Armagh, is posing as salesman, while his sister represents Ireland and begs her brother not to barter away the stone. An earnest advocate is about to strike the doctor a blow, which does not fall because of timely assistance.

I thought of getting a more savage Irishman to handle the stick; but, on reflection, concluded it might be better to get a mild specimen, for fear that Pat might think it would make it more realistic to deal the blow, or try his valor on the slender youth who dared to interfere. The picture is not so striking as it would have been in that case, but it was the striking part that I wanted to avoid. As it is, the picture will be looked at in sober earnest by some of the lower classes, and they will say that they would have done without any poteen for half a day to have had the chance the fellow had in the picture. An Irishman would rather fight than eat when he has little hunger and a good chance to try his muscular power. He will knock his friend down, and wonder, when he becomes irritated about it, that he does not know how to take a joke.

The picture is an excellent one of the castle, and I am sure that the reader will forgive me for not taking a larger man to restrain from an act of violence.

The stone is the lowest one in a projection of the wall, near the top. This projection extends about the tower, and is supported by stone brackets, as distinctly seen in the engraving. This outer wall is about six feet in height, and was used for a double defense when the enemy sought to attack the castle. Between the top of the main wall and this projected wall there is an opening the width of the brackets, which is about three feet. The defenders of the castle could stand safe from attack, and drop stones on the heads of the assailants who came near the walls. The stone may be seen near the center of this outer projected wall, and is the lowest stone of it, directly above the windows. To kiss it, one had to be held by the feet, and even then reach out the full length

BUYING BLARNEY CASTLE.

of the bracket. A few years ago a man lost his life in attempting to kiss the stone. Another foolish fellow made a similar effort, and fell on the bushes below, and escaped with a broken ankle. Kissing may be very pleasant, but it has not always been safe. But now a few iron bars have been put across the opening, and anyone who has sufficient faith may sink on bended knee, and lowering his head in a very humble way, kiss at pleasure, for the stone is too unsophistical to protest. But it is a favor that requires you to get on your knees before it will be granted. Sir Walter Scott visited the castle and kissed the stone when it meant some risk to accomplish the task.

I suppose that in this, as in the social kiss, there may be various reasons assigned for the indulgence. Some kiss for fun, and others in deep earnest, but it is not probable that anyone kisses the stone out of sheer hypocrisy. Different accounts are given of the origin of the custom, and of the power of the stone to give eloquence and grace to the lips. A name would not have been attached to the castle without some reason, and that which is most probable is, that the old lord who owned the castle was away from home when his enemy came and demanded its surrender. There were not enough retainers left to hold out against the foe. The wife of the lord therefore tried her skill in flattering the enemy. She made them fair promises, and secured a delay of the hostilities. Day after day she renewed her pleas to the demand for surrender, always praising the gallantry and good looks of the enemy. She carried her point, and kept off the day of battle until her lord returned and defeated the enemy, whom she had deceived. Thus the castle was called Blarney, and the word has passed into common use. It is true that some try to attribute it to a form of a French word, signifying falsehood, but its real significance and use come from the castle. How the notion of becoming gifted by kissing the stone arose no one knows, and while few have any faith in the process, many tourists use the means and then go home to talk as bitterly as before.

But, after all, there is a lesson here that it might be well for us to learn. Men and women are seldom driven, but may be persuaded. The one of harsh and sarcastic speech will be avoided by those who care for their own comfort. "A soft answer turneth away wrath." A harsh answer may provoke a blow. Others may learn not to be deceived by fair speeches and promises. Many a modern Delilah has won the heart of a great Samson, and then shaved off his locks and turned the Philistines loose on him.

I was seriously rebuked by a lady, for kissing the Blarney stone. " It was vulgar and dangerous. Think

how many people have kissed the stone just where you
did! Ugh! It makes the cold chills run over me to
think of it. Disease is communicated in that way,
and I fear that evil results may follow." Then she
thought to soften her rebukes, and tone her indignation
down a little, and added: "In your case, too, it was
so absurd. You know, or ought to know that, for all
your friends know that you have not the least occasion
to resort to any extraordinary means to secure sweetness of speech!" I sat and listened, while she made
change with the conductor. Without ever regarding
the sacredness of her own lips, and considering the
danger of bacteria, she whipped out a dime, in place
of a nickel, and putting the coin in her mouth, held it
between her teeth! How the chills ran over me! A
microscope might have revealed ten thousand bacteriæ,
or animalculæ, or bacilli, or some other "a" or "i,"
skipping off the dime, and exploring the hidden
sweetness of her dainty little mouth. The conductor
took the dime in his rough hand, and put it into his
old pocket, among a pile of similar pieces, ready to be
taken between the lips of some fastidious party who
would not endanger her life by kissing a stone that is
washed by the perpetual showers of Ireland. I advise
all young men, before sealing the engagement, to make
sure that their chosen partners have not carried filthy
lucre between their teeth, however much they may

be pleased to know that they have it deposited in bank.

We were anxious to have our pictures finished, to bring with us, and I consented to remain, and let the artist and our friends go in the jaunting car. I found a little hotel, where a number of strangers were taking lunch, and, after listening to their conversation, went out to find that our joke was liable to become more serious than we had intended. I was asked to reveal the object of our visit, and what was the meaning of the talk of taking away the stone. I remembered the story of Mrs. McCarthy keeping the enemy out of the castle until her lord came home, and began telling them about America, and their friends there, until the train came up, and thus escaped from danger, real or imagined.

The next morning the doctor remembered that he had considerable shopping to do. He was to bring souvenir spoons from Paris, and London, and Venice, and a half-dozen other cities. He had to bring home treasures from Switzerland, and Italy, and Germany. We tried to shop. But everything was Irish. Every piece of jewelry had shamrocks on it; every souvenir spoon had shamrocks on it. There was nothing Italian or French to be had. We were at our wits' end. I suggested that we buy all our friends shillelahs, but he thought it might be better not to tempt them.

We went from one shop to another, seeking something to suit the individual necessities with more eagerness than ever Saul sought for his father's asses.

We found it difficult to remember what stores we had been in. We asked for breastpins, and rings, and spoons, and knives and forks, and lace handkerchiefs, and gloves. We exhausted our shopping vocabulary. I told the doctor he ought to have taken my advice, and filled up his trunk with wooden shoes. Then we made the rounds again, but everything was Irish. In despair, we bought several packages of cholera mixture, for which the doctor had given a prescription. But these were not suitable for presents. We relieved the tedium of looking, by occasionally buying a half-dozen handkerchiefs, or a few pairs of socks. Then we would go back to the jewelry stores, and buy another spoon with shamrocks on it. The only things we had that were certainly proper for presents we collected during the last hour. They were two Irish blackthorns, a little pot of shamrock, and a crock of ivy.

I will never be a successful shopper. It takes more tact than I can command. When in London, the doctor told me that he wished I would buy something for one of his friends. I thought, now I will astonish him. I asked a couple of American ladies of excellent taste, if they would go shopping with me.

They consented. The mother and daughter both said they would go. Now, I will succeed. I have the taste of the middle-aged and the young. We went to a great store on Regent Street.

"Did you ever go shopping?"

"No, I never did. Is it pleasant? Are the shop-keepers glad to see you?"

"O, certainly they will be glad; but it is not necessary to take things because they have shown them to you."

"But suppose that they tell me this is what I want, will I not take it?"

"Not at all. You are supposed to know what suits you, better than any stranger."

"But, forgive me for suggesting that they have more experience." I promised that I would not buy anything simply because the shop-keeper said it was the proper thing for me. How polite the gentleman was who met us at the door! He bowed, and asked what he could show us. I supposed he wanted to sell, but he said he wanted to show anything. He took us to a counter, and a lady about forty-five, who was dressed as though she were twenty, smiled on us and began to exhibit things.

"This, I know, will suit you."

I was going to take it on her recommendation, when I saw the ladies smiling to each other. I wanted to be suited. I consulted the ladies, and they said we had better look some place else. The lady returned with something that was "the prettiest thing in London." I knew that was what we wanted, but told her that we need not take things simply because she had shown them to us, and that shop-keepers were pleased to exhibit their goods whether customers bought or not. She wanted to know how I knew this, and I looked at the ladies, who were smiling, as much as to say, "It will be all right to tell her," and so I told her that I had never been shopping before in my life, but that the ladies had told me this, and I knew it must be so.

They all laughed. I told her then that her goods were very pretty, but we would look around a little, and if we did not find anything that pleased us as well as her goods did, we would return. Would she lay aside the goods for us? It was hardly worth while to do this, for it was as easy for her to get them out of the case, as it would be to look them up if she put them away.. She did not smile at this, but said she hoped to see us again.

The ladies told me that I would be a splendid shopper, but that it might be well for me not to be so confidential on short acquaintance.

We visited several other stores and then held a council, at which it was unanimously agreed that we could do better at the first place than anywhere we

19

had been.   As we returned, the ladies said that the shop-lady would be glad to see me.   She did not say this when we came to her counter again; and so I asked her if she was, and she replied, "I am delighted."   I now knew that the ladies who were with me were wiser than I was.   I went on and told the saleslady that we had been ever so many places, and had returned to take her goods, and that it was a far higher compliment to her to come back and buy the things we had looked at before, than it would have been for us to have taken them at first sight!   At this all the ladies laughed, and the seller of the goods said we certainly had shown good taste!   How easy it is for people to give compliments when they are merited.   My friends complimented me on the attainments I had made and said I should not go by myself to buy anything; that they could get a whole party to go with me.   But I did not see the need of having so many to counsel when the shop-keepers were willing to advise you what to buy.

But this is a digression.   The doctor thought we could get all the other foreign goods in New York, and save duties.   I was so sorry that we did not begin extensive shopping sooner.   It is educational, and tests our merits and graces to the utmost.   At this writing, one month after our return, the ivy has gone with the twining woodbine.   One sprig of shamrock is struggling for life, but its breathing is not satisfactory. The black-thorn canes are still in our possession, and will likely remain with us, as nobody was willing to accept them. We can replace the ivy somewhere in Chicago, and no one can prove that it did not come from Ireland. I do not wonder that ladies do so much shopping. It is a delight; a joy; a refreshing!

We heard the far-famed bells of Shandon and recalled the words of Francis Mahoney :

> With deep affection
> And recollection,
> I often think of those Shandon bells ;
> Whose sounds so wild, would,
> In the days of my childhood,
> Fling around my cradle their magic spells.

But we failed to recognize any particular charm in their tolling, even when " on the waters of the River Lee." But I have believed for a long time that our appreciation depends very much on the relation we sustain to the one who speaks or sings, or to the bell that rings. There is also a good degree of poetic license taken with the truth in the lines quoted. Mahoney must have been a remarkable baby, if, when writhing with colic, or cutting teeth in his cradle, there were any magic spells thrown about him by the church bells.

We went to Queenstown by boat, thus obtaining a sight of the River Lee, with its green, sloping banks. It was a fitting close to a journey through Ireland.

Queenstown has a magnificent harbor; large enough, it is claimed, to hold the combined navies of the world. It is fortified, and, to some extent, undermined in such a way as to render a near approach by hostile vessels very dangerous. But, with present armaments, a vessel could besiege the city successfully, at a distance too great to be hindered by guns on land.

We saw some peculiar developments of the Irish life — the abject poverty of the poor and the shrewdness of the well-to-do. Miserable-looking women, half clad, and in their bare feet, begging with the utmost persistency that you buy a little shamrock, or some pipes or canes from them. They follow you persistently for blocks, and are ready to greet you at every crossing. It is this class, that have come to America in such numbers, that have given grossly false impressions of the Irish character and people. The representatives, true representatives of Ireland, who have not been degraded by superstition and debauched by rum, are a most generous, large-hearted, clear-minded people. Their wit is proverbial, and their impulses are noble.

Even among the poor classes this holds true. I was resting quietly on the steps of the Queen's Hotel **the** evening before our departure, when a fine-looking fellow drove up with his jaunting car, and in the most polite manner possible invited me to ride with him. I answered, laughingly, that I had spent a great deal of money already and must begin to economize.

"Well, sir," said he, "I am a poor man, but I would never think of charging so fine a looking gintleman! You can ride with me an hour and I will not charge you a penny."

"But I do not see how you can afford this, and I would not be willing to take your time and tire out your horse when you might have someone able and willing to pay you."

"Ah! Colonel," said he, "I am selfish, like the rest of the world. I know it will pay me. It will set off my car so to have you in it, that everyone will want to ride in the same car that the handsome American gintleman used! I tell you, Colonel, I could make a fortune if I had a man like you to ride with me a little while every day!"

Here was an opportunity to help the poor fellow, but two considerations kept me back. Why did he take me for a Colonel? He ought to have thought me a General! I told him that there are said to be many temptations in the way of the rich, and that it might be better for him and me to remain poor. Of course this fellow knew that after one had ridden with him

he would be sure of his pay.   But he has made many
a shilling by his flatteries.

It was a great pleasure, next morning, to see our
ship steaming into the harbor.   As soon as she was
sighted, a flag was run up to the mast of the tender, and
we took our black-thorns, ivy, and shamrock, and got
aboard.   As we neared the ship we recognized some
friends whom we had met on the continent.   There
were also many distinguished Americans aboard—
editors, ministers, authors, historians, tragedians,
teachers, singers, and artists.   But all were resting.
The preachers had no opportunity to exercise their
gifts, owing to the rigid rules of the company, or
officers, who permitted nothing but the reading of the
services of the Church of England ; the singers would
not spoil their voices by using them in the salôn ;
the pianists would not play on an instrument so badly
out of tune ; the actors would not risk their reputations,
and so a dull concert was the only entertainment
afforded.

It was cold, damp, and dreary, most of the way.
The fog-horn kept blowing for hours and the passengers cheered each other up by talking about the
cholera, and the prospects of many days of quarantine,
and the delights of fumigation.   The ladies were more
highly favored than the gentlemen, for in rough
weather they had a little parlor to which they could

go ; but the gentlemen were shut up in their state-rooms
or in a dingy little saloon where smoking and gam-
bling were in order by day and by night.

When the storm abated, the voyage became tolera-
ble, and the tables appeared more cheerful. Men
exercised their skill playing at shuffle-board, and many
pale-faced passengers appeared on deck. Their features plainly revealed the struggles of the past few days.

Two days before reaching New York a land bird
came on deck. It had been driven out by the storm,
and was nearly exhausted when it found a refuge on
the ship. There was much sympathy expressed for
this lost wanderer, and one of the sailors played Noah
and took it in where food and water were given it.
Its necessity made it tame and willing to trust its fate
to the hands of men. Its confidence was not misplaced,
nor would it have been safe for anyone to have treated
the tired bird with cruelty. There is a tender spot in
every human heart, if we only had the skill to touch it;
but the strange spectacle may be presented of men
and women showing kindness to a bird and neglecting
a brother or sister. How many of these have been
driven out by storms against which they were not able
to stand, and no refuge was near them, and no kind
hand was reached out to take them in. A land bird
many hundreds of miles out on the waters, compelled
to fly by day and night, its wings weary, its feathers

wet, hungry and thirsty, and sleepy, calls forth our sympathies. No rough questions are asked of it about its coming here. No one says, " Why did you not stay on shore?" We are not always so considerate with our fellow mortals and the rude question reveals the spirit in which it is asked. Poor prodigal, what made you leave your home? Why do you not go back again? Ah! there was a storm, and for a little while it seemed so pleasant to be borne along with it, and at last return became impossible!

The sight of land came while we slept. We were near the shore, but were all unconscious of the fact. During the darkness the engines that had been pulsating for eight days ceased to throb.

We were lying at anchor in the upper quarantine. The morning dawned and eager watchers looked out toward the islands. A few minutes more and we would have been at the dock, but we were in quarantine. A boat belonging to the health department came near. We held a hurried consultation. The tenor of it was about this: We have come from a healthy port; we have no sickness on board; we have a clean bill of health, and now an officer comes from New York, where there is cholera; will it not be wise for us to lower a life-boat and meet him and see that he is duly fumigated before we permit him to come on the vessel?

In half an hour he left us again and came back three hours later. It was very unsatisfactory to be kept in ignorance. Another boat came near and gave us our mail and daily papers.

We were left to read and discuss the news and the prospect of getting off. We began to sympathize with the *Roumania* passengers, who had been treated like wild beasts or lepers. The health officers took our statements about where we had been during the last ten days, and then left us, saying that a few pieces of baggage that had been in Paris must be fumigated. They returned late in the afternoon, and sprinkled a disinfectant on the outside of a couple of trunks and left us again.

One incident alone relieved the monotony of the day. A lady passenger from New York had a little pre-arranged signal with her husband, who had returned home before her. The lady stood on deck with her two little children, eagerly looking out to the island above Fort La Fayette. She would look through the field-glasses, and then return to her chair, only to rise and look again. At last she was rewarded for her patience. A gentleman appeared on the far-off island slope and waved two handkerchiefs. He held one in each hand and waved them. Then he looked at us through a glass. The passengers stood back, so as to leave the lady alone. She took a handkerchief in each hand and waved them to her husband. Then she took the children and held them in her arms while the little fellows waved, and kissed their hands to papa. Thus the performance went on for half an hour, but the signals were understood. Wife and children had seen husband and father on the shore waiting for them. The husband and father had seen his wife and children on the anchored vessel. Love had invented a signal service of its own, and could now await the hour when fond hopes would be realized.

It was dark when we were released and stepped out on solid land again, but this time the land was our own dear native land. Westward to the city by the lake we bore our treasures, and with satisfaction gave up the care of our ivy, and shamrock, and black-thorns.

"How did you feel when you saw your native land again?" May I turn to the first pages of these wanderings for an answer? One can not well answer. Ask the preacher how he felt when, after delivering his first sermon, the people invited him to become their pastor. Ask the physician how he felt when his first patient was recovered, and paid him his bill. Ask the lawyer how he felt when, after making his first speech to a jury, he heard them give in a verdict for his client. Ask your brother-in-law how he felt when your sister did not reject his proposal! Those old travelers who go to Europe every year without seeing anything have lost the delightful sensations that come to us when we are for the first time "home again, from a foreign shore." This is one of the joys we had not estimated when we left home. It can not be forecast. I had not dared think of it. It came with all the suddenness of the light that astonishes the child when the dark canvas is illuminated with the magnificent picture of the stereopticon. It had in it the calm, sweet, peaceful assurance of the bow on the cloud when the storm has passed away. Oh! the bliss of a new experience, that is a double delight because of our inexperience!

Our wanderings through Europe have passed into history. But let no one say that the memory of these pleasures is all that is left us now. There are chords in the human soul, that, when once touched, will never cease to vibrate. Warm greetings from loved ones, who, like myself, had considered the months of separation very long, convince me that "the best part of going away, is the coming back again!"

The summer months were gone and the fruits of autumn gathered in when the wanderer came home, and, with a grateful heart, stood once more before his people and looked again into their faces full of tender sympathy, and saw within the sacred place — not the less sacred because of its presence—the Banner of the American Republic.

LUCILE VERNON

OR

The Church at Lansington

.... BY ....

THE REV. W. T. MELOY, D. D.

PASTOR OF THE FIRST UNITED PRESBYTERIAN CHURCH, CHICAGO, ILL.

12 Mo.; 208 Pages. Portrait and Illustrations. Handsomely bound in Cloth. Third Edition.

PRICE 60 CENTS.

NOTICES OF THE PRESS.

The author shows his power of touching hearts in this description of the scene after the wedding: "Mr. Vernon sat down in his house, and bowing his white head, allowed unbidden tears to flow. Then he rose and walked through the different apartments of his dwelling, and said aloud: 'This is, after all, only a house. Once it was a bright and happy home, but now it is only a large, elegant, dreary house. One by one the lights have gone out. I long for what is seldom found this side the grave—rest.'"

JANE GREY SWISSHELM, in the Chicago (Ill.) *Advance.*

We congratulate the author on this literary lily of the valley.—*The Interior.*

"It is splendid" said Mrs. Ekin, as she finished reading LUCILE VERNON last evening. "Money paid for such books is a good investment." I fully concur with my wife's views. I trust LUCILE may find a place in every family. Let it have a wide circulation. I commend it with the greatest pleasure and satisfaction.

JAS. A. EKIN, *Late Dep'y Q. M. Gen'l U. S. Army.*

Address, inclosing Thirty (2 cent) Stamps,

W. T. MELOY

149 SOUTH PAULINA STREET, CHICAGO.